Coming Again is the exciting sequel to the original novel, *Coming About*. Both books were first serialized in *Tidewater Times*.

Praise for *Coming About*

Binged the last two nights, richly enjoying your book. I congratulate you on putting together a "sailing novel" which satisfies the likes of me, but is in fact more human drama. Nice bits, over and over! very worldly and crafty as hell.

As I read description of Isha, and later Becky, I mused on how you might have enjoyed envisioning, then listing those (considerable) attributes.

Very nice work.

~ Warwick Tompkins

It's rare that an author has both the sailing knowledge and the literary chops to pull off a compelling, modern day novel set around sailing . . .but Roger Vaughan has the unique background to pull it off. Come for the sailing and stay for the story.

~ Erin L. Schanen, editor, *SAILING*

The Roger Vaughan Library

COMING AGAIN

A Novel

BY ROGER VAUGHAN

Choptank Word Bank

The Roger Vaughan Library

Published by Choptank Word Bank
Bachelor's Point, Oxford, Maryland
www.choptankwordbank.com

ISBN 978-1-7333135-6-8
Library of Congress Control Number: 2023907359

Cover Photograph: Gilles Martin-Raget

Cover and Interior Design: Joseph Daniel
www.storyartsmedia.com

POD Edition
Printed in the United States

For Kippy

Table of Contents

I

ESCAPE

The handcuffs hurt.

They weren't really handcuffs. They were wire-ties that law enforcement was using: mean, thin but tough plastic bands designed to wrap bulky bundles of wires. They prove very damaging to one's wrists if they are put on too tightly, and they are always put on too tightly. The least bit of struggle causes painful chafing and blood. But they do have one advantage, Isha thought, trying to find the most comfortable position for her bound wrists as the officers led her into the elevator. The ties calmed her down, creating enough discomfort that her blind fury was reduced to a level where her more rational self could preside over the situation. That was good, because rational was required.

Her calm had started with the detective, that large, cool hunk of African manhood who had moved that bitch

Becky off her and had gently drawn her to her feet by one arm as if she were a feather. Becky had blindsided her when Isha had gone for the gun. The detective had read her Miranda rights quietly, with meaning, as if it were a poem. His eyes were powerful, stern and controlling without being threatening. She admittedly had been transfixed by him.

There would be plenty of time to be furious, plenty of time to vent the rage that comes from failure, the deep-seated anger that follows a devious plan gone wrong; plenty of time to nourish the vicious revenge that was already growing like a tumor in her heart. She'd been through several ugly years of scheming and pretending, being charming to idiots, jumping into bed with creeps, all to end up in handcuffs thanks to an incompetent partner who couldn't get his side of the job done, thanks to the clever little bastard son he had underestimated. Whom she had underestimated. She had to share that part. When you can blame it on someone else, that dilutes some of the curse. But when you have to take some of the blame, when it's your fuckup— well, that's the worst, the very worst.

She'd done her job. She'd had Andy wrapped around her little finger. She had. No question. At first, anyway. It was textbook stuff. Anything she wanted he got for her, including her pair of world-class breasts. Not that they weren't prizewinning to begin with. But now they were impossible to ignore. Andy was putty in her hands, nothing a little time between the sheets couldn't fix if things got testy, with the emphasis on little. Portion it out, like candy to a baby. Poor confused Andy, angry Andy, poor rich white boy. Just give him another drink, roll him another joint, buy him another toy. Such a simple mommy's boy. And then what happened? He had started to think! She had seen it that night when he caught her going through his Mountain View plans, that stupid astronomy-themed hotel idea of his. She'd heard the wheels turning, seen it in his eyes, and she had let it go, not given it the attention it deserved. Thinking, for chrissakes. Is there anything more dangerous? And she had let it go.

It was that goddamn ocean race around the world. It had to be. Mitch's obsession with making Andy go on The Race had really blown the entire scam. Mitch and his infantile need to punish Andy after Andy's drunken gaffe at the New York Yacht Club had forced Mitch's hand, a gaffe that had forced Mitch into entering a boat in The Race. Upward of $15 million it had cost the company. That bit of pocket change wasn't really the problem. It was the old baggage, rotten to the core. Mitch had always hated the kid, the issue of his wife Deedee's one mistake in her otherwise pristine life: getting knocked up by her father's boat captain, some New Zealand dude. And that crippling business of Deedee's half-witted father sending the boat captain packing and insisting his daughter marry Mitch, his ambitious protégé in the company. "Bastard," Mitch called Andy, often to his face. Andy might have been a bastard, but he was in line to inherit the company, screwing Mitch out of what he thought should be his. Mitch had actually tried to have Andy killed once, arranged to have a couple of toughs shoot him in a tunnel, stupid Mitch who couldn't wait to hand her over to the cops as the evil witch behind the plot. What a hideous oaf, so blinded by greed. How many times, after sex with him, had she dashed into the bathroom and thrown up?

And then there was Deedee, standing firmly behind Andy going on The Race. Who had known that would happen? Mother Deedee, who always bailed Andy out, who had saved his butt time after time. Not this time. Turned out Deedee, who was still in love with the boat captain, figured going on The Race was the way to make Andy get connected to his roots, and was betting he'd respond to the challenge. Talk about a long shot. But damned if the old lady wasn't right. Faced with having to race 30,000 miles around the world with eleven strangers on a stripped-out race boat had turned him around, turned fat into muscle, forged anger and fear into commitment, and made him start to think.

Andy was on The Race, all right. Or he should have been. It had been Mitch's idea to bring everything to a head during the race layover after the finish of a leg in Fremantle, Western Australia. Give Deedee her terminal cocktail. That would bring Andy home. Overcome with grief, he would be a piece of cake for Mitch's thugs. How wrong could he be — and she had gone along with it. Impatient Mitch. Isha letting her guard down. She knew better. Rage began boiling again in her guts.

The elevator door slid open. The cops flanking her each gave a pull, causing the cuffs to punish her wrists. She had better start to think. The two cops, one a woman, guided her into the handsome lobby of the posh apartment building on Manhattan's Central Park West, where she and Mitch had been living. Ralph, the night doorman, was stunned by the sight of his fantasy woman in custody. Ralph's building had its fair share of gorgeous women, but this one was something else, a Black-Asian mix underpainted with a liberal dose of Caucasian. The result was sultry to the max, with those big, wide-set eyes and that full, expressive mouth so striking in a girlish face framed by the perfectly tousled hair. Uncanny. And that body that defied gravity . . . She was small, not a fraction over five feet three, which advanced a certain innocence that Isha always made the most of. And here she was, in handcuffs! Isha gave Ralph her best bedraggled look, eyes sad as she mouthed, "It's okay, a mistake." The cops were about to take her to the local precinct while Andy and the detectives were still upstairs dealing with Mitch.

Isha stopped abruptly, causing the wire ties to dig into her wrists. "I need a toilet," Isha mumbled to the woman officer. "Now. I'm about to burst." It was an old ruse, but never a bad one. And probably the only one available. The delivery was everything. Isha bent over and produced a wet, throaty cough, pressing her hands to her stomach.

"You can make it to the station," the male officer interjected. "It's ten minutes." His name tag read "Quimby."

"I will foul myself and your car," Isha said, casting an imploring look in Ralph's direction. "I am ill."

"She could use the little service toilet down the hall." It was Ralph, eager to help his favorite tenant. Isha let her head drop. She appeared in obvious distress.

The woman cop looked at her partner, who had rank. He grimaced.

"All right. Damn. Hurry it up."

Ralph led the way. The woman officer kept a hand on Isha's arm. Outside the toilet door, Isha held her cuffed wrists up to the officer.

"I'll need my hands."

The woman officer opened the toilet door and glanced inside at the tiny, windowless room with a toilet and a utility sink. A broom and a mop stood in a bucket. There was barely room for one person.

The officer, Gaines, cast a glance over her shoulder, removed a set of clippers from her belt, and cut the wire ties. Later, under questioning, Gaines would tell her angry superiors that while it was true Isha had tried to unholster Quimby's gun during the arrest, and while she'd had a screaming fight with Andy's girlfriend, Becky, who had tackled her, she had been totally subdued in the lobby. She had appeared nauseated, sick. And how could she do her business with her hands tied?

After three minutes, Gaines would urge Isha to hurry it up. At five minutes, Gaines would begin pounding on the locked toilet door. At ten minutes, Quimby would attempt to kick the door in, injuring his foot. At twelve minutes, Ralph would find the key and unlock the door to the toilet room, which was empty. The grid to the heat vent was lying on the floor. The opening seemed impossibly small, but Isha had never weighed more than a hundred pounds. Quimby pressed Ralph about where the heat duct led, and Gaines ran off in that direction. She was too late. Isha had kicked her way out and was gone.

After exiting the apartment building's back entrance and running up the alley to the street, Isha had hailed a taxi. It was good luck that she had her wallet in the pocket of the jeans she was wearing. Before the police had arrived, she'd gone out for ice cream. She gave the driver a hundred-dollar bill and told him he needed to cruise around for an hour. Where he went was up to him. She curled up on the seat out of sight and dozed, considering her options.

An hour later she directed the driver to cruise by the apartment building. It was now around 1:00 a.m. The place looked quiet. No suspicious-looking cars. On the next pass she stopped the cab. Ralph came out, his face full of concern.

"They're gone," he said. "They taped off your door."

Isha asked the driver to wait in the back, where he had picked her up. The driver took in the building, the doorman, who obviously knew this woman, and said he would.

"It's a colossal mistake," Isha said to Ralph. "Our lawyers are already on it. This is going to cost the city plenty. Help me out, and you'll be taken care of."

"Of course, ma'am."

"I'm not here. You have not seen me. I need a key."

"Got it," Ralph said, disappearing for a moment into his cubby by the front door as Isha headed for the elevator. Ralph returned with the key. Isha stared into Ralph's eyes, grabbed the lapels of his uniform coat, and put her cheek against his chest. His arms automatically went around her.

"Thank you, Ralph. You are such a good man."

Ralph could hardly speak. "Anything . . . just call," he managed.

This was almost as good as hiding at the police station, Isha thought, stifling a rueful laugh as the elevator door slid shut. The tape on the apartment door was for show. She'd leave it just as she found it. She took her time shedding her clothes, filthy from crawling through the heat ducts, showering, and dressing in a late-night, Lower Manhattan street outfit for November: jeans, a black cashmere turtleneck, and warm, flat boots. She'd wear her three-quarter-length black down coat that could be squashed into a tiny bag and a dark designer stocking cap.

Isha packed one of her larger roller suitcases, selecting a variety of outfits for both winter and warmer climes, along with jewelry and accessories. She'd considered getting a night's sleep and venturing off in the morning, but decided not to push it. They had taken Mitch's computers, but the cops would want to tear the place apart come morning. She went to the safe and removed several thousand dollars in cash her partner kept on hand, muttering a sarcastic "Thanks, Mitch." She grabbed the spare mobile phone they kept in the safe and a couple of computer discs that had to be valuable, put her wallet and a few essentials in a canvas tote bag, grabbed the roller bag, and took the freight elevator down to avoid Ralph.

The taxi was waiting. "Chelsea Hotel," she told the driver.

II

GRADY

The phone rang. Andy watched him pick it up and answer it in that quiet, understated way he did everything: "Grady."

Grady Smith, his father at long last, in the flesh. And what a guy, a marvelous reality after twenty-odd years of living with the lie that the vile Mitchell Thomas was his father. Mitchell, the man who had murdered Deedee, his mother; the man who had tried to kill him a couple of times and who was now locked in prison for the rest of his miserable life. Andy sincerely and unflinchingly hoped it would be miserable.

Andy took a sip of his Victoria Bitter and watched Grady get up from his chair and walk slowly away, trailing the extra-long telephone cord behind him. He liked calling him Grady. It was a little late for "Father." He sure looked good for sixty: fit, spare-framed, balanced. He was just under six feet tall and had a thick head of hair, blond going white around the edges. His face was weather-beaten, an occupational hazard. Grady had always been a boat guy. He still was, far as Andy knew.

Once again Andy took in the living room of this waterfront pad that was part of a boatyard south of the Sydney Harbour Bridge. It was meant to provide a no-frills emergency overnight for customers, but Grady had scored it. The boatyard owner was a mate. There was nothing much to it: living room, bathroom, bedroom, galley, altogether smaller than the accommodations on a forty-footer. But the location couldn't be beat if you enjoyed being around boats. There was a view of the bridge out the bedroom window. It was a little noisy during the day, but it was friendly noise: grinders, sanders, travel-lift and crane motors. If you liked boats. Grady was bicoastal, Andy had found out, commuting between this small apartment here in Sydney and similar digs in Fremantle in Western Australia. Grady was a bit of a mystery, but then they had just gotten started.

The last leg, around the South Coast of Australia to Sydney, had been mostly boring, slow, giving credence to the claim that 70 percent of ocean racing is likely to be sailed in light to moderate conditions. While not as dangerous or physical, light air is just as hard on a crew as a gale, with the constant sail changes required and the need to pore over weather faxes trying to figure out where wind might be hiding until one can hardly see, or think. Sailing in gales is at least exciting. You might be cold and exhausted, but flying along at twenty knots or more also means you are getting somewhere, fast. Watching the speedo registering between three and six knots day after day is depressing. It tests one's concentration, and temper. And if it is hot, the crew is in shorts and bare feet most of the time. Without wind, the combination of damp sails, cooking smells, and sweaty bodies makes below decks rank.

All American had done well, winning the last leg over skipper Jan Sargent's Kiwi rival, Alistair Koonce, skippering *Ram Bunctious*, by half a day. By the looks, it was going to be a two-boat race, which wasn't unusual. In addition to frustrating the sailors, light wind separates a fleet. The luck factor goes up in light air from around 15 percent under moderate conditions (ten to fifteen knots of wind, reasonable sea state) to 30 percent or even more. Boats just half a mile apart can be sailing in different wind conditions. Light wind is the enemy of close finishes. And light wind is fickle, often turning what would seem to be a brilliant strategy into a bad call.

Andy had done most of the talking with Grady so far. Replaying the leg from Fremantle had taken a while. Andy had kept *All American* off the beach, as Grady had suggested. Way off. Andy, skipper Jan Sargent, and Damaris, the navigator, had taken *All American* twenty miles offshore, a brave move that had finally paid off. After initially falling behind by thirty-five miles to several boats that had chosen the beach route, they'd found a small weather system they were able to stay in. That had given them a big boost. Grady had dug out a chart and wanted details about their track, and about the previous leg into Fremantle, when Andy had bet on the famous Fremantle

Doctor, a strong onshore breeze that comes up on schedule many afternoons, and won. Andy relived it for Grady, who was all ears.

After that, Andy had done his best to recap the last twenty-five years for his father. He was in the middle of that when the phone rang. Grady was a good listener. He had known about Mitch, although he'd never met him. Like Andy, he was a big fan of Ossie, Karl Oyslebow, who had been maintaining the family's boats since Andy's grandfather had hired him long ago. Grady wasn't surprised that Ossie wouldn't talk to Andy about his mother. Ossie knew everything, but Deedee's father had saved him from being jailed, or perhaps deported. Ossie had made a mess of a guy who had threatened him in a Newport, Rhode Island, bar one night, back when trendy America's Cup Avenue was called Thames Street, back when all of Thames Street had smelled like stale beer. After Ossie had put the guy in the hospital, the great designer Nat Herreshoff, Ossie's employer, had called Deedee's father, Randolph Moss. Without Moss's intervention, and his subsequent employment of Ossie, the tough Norwegian would have been toast. No matter what Randolph had done, Ossie would never have given him up, or shared any family secrets. That was how he was.

Mention of Randolph had gotten Grady talking. "It took me a long while to figure out that miserable son of a bitch," Grady said. "Such a powerful guy, brilliant, inventor of that big lens that made him a massive fortune. Eccentric, for sure. Hated cars. Worked nights, and those elves . . ." Grady shook his head. "Randolph really did believe a bunch of elves showed him how to make that lens. But so insecure, socially. Damn odd. He had everything to make him a supremely confident person — talent, accomplishment, tons of money — but he was never comfortable in his own skin. Extremely insecure to a sick degree. Obsessed with what people might think."

Andy was hesitant, but he waded in.

"How did he . . ."

"With threats. Bad threats. Threats I knew he meant."

"How bad?"

"Having me arrested for rape was one. Jail term guaranteed. And I'd always be known as a sex offender. But worse, he threatened to have the baby aborted. That would be you." Grady stared at his son.

Andy had a shiver. "But Deedee . . ."

"Wouldn't have mattered what Deedee said. He cowed people, Deedee especially. You only knew Deedee after Randolph had crippled her. She was something else before that. Great sailor. Great athlete. Knock your block off on the tennis court. Played field hockey too, lightning fast, great ball handler and scorer. Dug life. Great woman." The memory had stopped Grady. He'd looked away, rubbed his forehead, taken a few breaths.

"Sorry, man. It had to be awful."

"S'okay. You need to know, need to hear it, then we can put it back on the freaking shelf where it belongs. But yeah, it was bad. I still have days when I wonder what I should have done. Believe me, I thought of everything, including killing the crazy old son of a bitch. I might have enjoyed that. But I was nothing, his boat captain, the guy who knocked up his daughter, a foreigner without portfolio, not even a green card at the time. No leg to stand on. It would have been me against this wealthy, famous genius who wasn't just beyond the law. He was the law. And the idea that his daughter would have a lowly boat bum as a partner, let alone as a husband, was so far beneath him he couldn't imagine it. The social embarrassment he'd suffer was beyond his comprehension. He'd be ridiculed!"

Grady sipped his Bitter, visibly upset. Andy said nothing.

"My deal was: be on the next plane to Auckland. No goodbyes. Just disappear. Like one of those bad Western movies. Either that or he gets me arrested for rape and has the child aborted. That would have killed Deedee. It would have. What he did ruined her. I've often thought he might as well have killed her. Would have been more humane. But I couldn't participate in that."

Grady looked at Andy. "We loved each other, Deedee and me."

"I know." Andy paused. "Deedee wouldn't talk much, but toward the end she did tell me one thing that really hit home. She said when Randolph was on his deathbed, he called her in to tell her everything material was hers, but he couldn't leave her his 'gift' because he didn't want her to think she was as good as he was."

Grady shook his head. "That says it." He leaned back in his chair, craned his neck and studied the ceiling.

"What about her mother, my grandmother? All these years I never heard a word about her. No pictures in those scrapbooks Mother kept, lips buttoned if the subject ever came up. Of course, it never came up . . ."

"Helena. She was long gone. She'd walked out on Randolph when Deedee and her brother were toddlers.

Couldn't take all the weirdness, him working in the dark hours like a bat, treating his kids like science experiments, eating only half-cooked beef, never a vegetable — he said the cows ate plenty of greens — and who knows what he demanded in bed. Helena never told. But she just took a car and left one night with her toothbrush and the clothes on her back. His people chased her down, made her sign a bunch of papers, gave her a bunch of money. Part of the deal was, she had to disappear quietly. And she did, according to Deedee. Said she never heard from Helena. Wouldn't know where to find her."

Andy looked quizzically at Grady.

"Oh yeah, I also had a contract. I was to disappear, never to be in touch with Deedee, never to mention my job with Randolph, never this, never that, or else. And here's something: he also gave me a check. Twenty grand. A lot of money back then. I refused it. He said I couldn't. It was part of the 'or else' deal. He said he wanted to be fair. Can you imagine? He wanted to be fair. Fair?!" Grady chuckled, head down, studied the floor. No answers there either.

Andy's mind was spinning. He knew full well his grandfather was strange, but this monstrous image of Randolph was frightening. The man really was twisted, not to mention obnoxious, and also dangerous. Whatever genius Randolph Moss had that enabled him to create the optics breakthrough that had made him famous had cost him dearly in human terms. The prodigy syndrome. Andy had a frightening thought about the nature of his own genes. He dared to hope Grady's influence on the biology had been dominant.

"But you knew about me," Andy said.

"I did. Deedee managed to get one letter out with a photo of baby Andy. She got one of the nurses to take a Polaroid, gave it to Myrtle, her faithful maid, with a letter. Sent it to a PO box I had in Auckland. It almost cost Myrtle her job. I heard it from Ossie through the yachting grapevine. Randolph had his suspicions, but could never prove it. That was lucky. He considered Myrtle a slave, three-fifths of a person. Probably would have tied her up in the garage and beaten her. That was the last I ever heard from Deedee."

"Jesus. But wait . . . that photo of the baby in the bathroom, that's me, baby Andy?"

"Yeah." Grady stifled a laugh. "Baby Andy."

"In the head?"

"Head's the best place for art or a photo you like. Captive audience in there. Got to give them something cool to study. Baby Andy, in this case."

That was when the phone had rung.

Andy went to the head again, mostly to have a closer look at the first photo of himself. The nurse had gotten an amusing baby picture. His eyes were open and on the camera. His little fists were clenched, and his toothless mouth was wide open in what could be construed as a laugh, but most probably it was a yawn. Or gas. It made Andy smile. He'd go with the laugh.

When he got back to the living room, Grady was off the phone, having opened a couple of new Bitters.

"Tell me about Isha," Grady said.

"She escaped," Andy said.

III

PATIENT NINA

The bus smelled bad. Isha caught herself, complaining about something so insignificant. Where she could have ended up would have smelled a lot worse, among other things. At least the bus was warm, and not too crowded. She was in a window seat, well screened by a large woman beside her on the aisle. Not that it really mattered. She felt safe. Over the past three weeks she had not sensed a single thread reaching out in her direction. She couldn't believe there hadn't been something, some little detail that could have given them a tiny lead. But apparently not. Maybe they simply didn't care, or had other things to do. And they had Mitch, had him for murder, smoking gun and all. Who was she, after all, compared to that prize fool.

She'd been at the Chelsea for three weeks, three incredibly boring weeks that had felt like three months.

Probably too soon to feel safe, clean, or ignored, but Isha's small ration of patience was getting stretched, and she was running low on money. She couldn't wait any longer. At first she'd thought it would have been so much better if it were summer, or even spring, but it turned out that winter, aside from the rotten weather, did have its advantages for what she had in mind. She hadn't done anything at the Chelsea except plan, sleep, plan, and eat the lightest meals possible.

The Chelsea, in Downtown Manhattan, long known as a haven for artists, musicians, actors, and various minor celebrities who wanted to be left alone, had been the perfect choice. She'd been hit on a few times, something she was used to, but her quietly expressed lack of interest served to quickly send the wannabes packing, and with apologies. The Chelsea aura was that powerful. She'd left the hotel infrequently, happy to take her meals in the restaurant at odd hours. And she looked quite different. She'd had her hair dyed blonde in a salon near the hotel, used a foundation cream to lighten her lovely tan complexion, and was always cautious. Bulky winter clothing provided a handy disguise on the streets.

She'd done a little shopping for basics she kept in the kitchenette of her room, and a few items of clothing. She'd taken the bus to the New York Public Library a few times in search of information she needed. Her Toshiba laptop was the latest model, but it hadn't been much help finding people. Working the telephone had proved to be the most productive.

Isha had dozed off. She awoke as the bus squealed to a stop at the Vince Lombardi rest area at the northern end of the New Jersey Turnpike. It was three days after Christmas, dark and chilly at six o'clock in the evening. Temperature was in the high thirties, not too bad. She zipped her down coat, picked up her only piece of luggage — a canvas shoulder bag — and went into the restaurant. It was crowded on this Sunday when people were traveling home from holiday pilgrimages.

Anyone watching this woman for the next two hours as she stood by the glass doors, focused on the parking lot, frequently dashing out to look at a particular car that had pulled in, would have been scratching their head. If they had been very observant, they would have noticed she was only interested in late-model, expensive cars. Even a trained observer wouldn't have gotten much beyond that. But her routine suddenly changed after she checked out a new Range Rover. She was out the door in a flash once she'd spotted the car and marked the driver. After having a quick look at the rear end of the car, she followed the driver into the restaurant. He went into the men's room. When he came out, he bought a coffee. That was when she struck.

Isha, who had unzipped her coat to reveal her well-filled-out beige cashmere turtleneck, draped with pearls and several gold chains upon which hung several handsome, jeweled trinkets, positioned herself just off the man's path to the doors. She had her mobile phone to her ear and was speaking loudly and hysterically into it as the driver of the Range Rover approached: "What in hell do you think you are doing! Come back here, David, goddamn it, you cannot do this! You have my bags! Come back! Hello? David?! You . . . Shit!" She flung the phone in anger, hitting the driver on the neck as he passed by, ten feet away.

Startled, the man reflexively spun away. His coffee spilled, some of it landing on his jacket. He turned to see this petite, gorgeous woman looking horrified at what she had just done. Isha was on him. "Oh my God, I am so sorry, oh my, please forgive me, that was so stupid, wait, I'll get some napkins . . ." She walked quickly around the corner to the cream-and-sugar stand. There was nothing for the driver to do but follow. First he retrieved Isha's phone. He was done for at that point.

The driver was in his fifties, a fit-looking man in khaki trousers, short, well-worn L.L. Bean boots, and what had to be an imported shearling quilted car coat. He had a healthy, outdoor look about him. Isha attacked the coffee stains on his coat with a bundle of napkins while talking a blue streak. "I am so sorry. I really lost it, please forgive me, I am frantic, I don't usually throw my telephone at people, really I don't. Oh my God . . ." The driver, who had yet to utter a word, handed Isha her phone.

"You okay?" he asked, quite engaged by this frenzied, tasty bundle of energy he had encountered.

Isha kept at the spilled coffee with a new bunch of napkins. "Oh yes, fine . . ." She paused. "No, actually, no, I'm not okay. Oh my God, what a mess." She stopped, the ball of soggy napkins clutched in her fist, looking dazed as the impossibility of her situation seemed to take hold.

"What's happened," the driver inquired, gently.

"I've been left," Isha said, choking back a sob. "Abandoned. We had a fight. Awful. Never mind. I'm very sorry."

"Is there someone you can call? A sister, a brother?"

"California." Isha's smile was wan.

The driver paused. "Could I drop you somewhere? I'm headed north, toward Larchmont, New York."

Isha knew. The Larchmont Yacht Club sticker on the Rover was why she had picked this guy. No sense prolonging it. "Oh my God, could you? Yes, oh, that would be a great help."

"I'm Cameron. Cam." He offered his hand.

"Nina," she said, taking it.

In the car, Isha met Chum, Cameron's black Labrador. Isha wasn't keen on dogs. A dog had never been a part of her life. Dogs scared her, if the truth were known. She avoided them. Chum was a big dog, but like most Labs he was easy with people. Friendly. He welcomed Isha to the car with a warm muzzle to her neck as she sat down. She gave a little shriek. Cameron chuckled, then suggested to Chum that he lie down. Chum did.

They talked. Isha related a sordid tale of a shaky relationship that had totally come to grief over a three-day Christmas visit to her fiancé's broken family; how his mother was mean as a cornered rat when she was drunk, which was anytime she was awake. Isha said the mother was a racist who considered Isha a rotten immigrant and hated her for trying to finesse her way into the family. And the father was a creep, also a drunk, though not as bad — and how he was grabbing her on the sly whenever he could, and how her fiancé wouldn't believe her.

Cameron shook his head and had to smile over what he said had to be a classic Christmas horror story, for sure one of the ugliest. Isha liked that. She began to think this guy had potential. She liked his humor, his sense of

Christmas as a prime time for disasters, and his attitude that indicated he preferred cleaning up whatever milk had spilled and getting on with it. Isha's initial, somewhat vague plan had been to get a ride into Connecticut, work an invitation to spend the night, then steal a car when the house was quiet and move on. Nina was suddenly considering other possibilities, or at least being open to other options. Her goal could be stated simply: revenge, with Andy and that bitch Becky as her objectives. How she would get there was more complicated. She had a few names and numbers — hence the focus on Larchmont as a stepping stone — but there were going to be lots of decisions required on the run. Making the most of opportunities would be critical.

Isha found out that Cameron had been to his brother's in Cape May, New Jersey, for Christmas. Nothing special. He said he did it every year and that it was reliably boring. He said he could have used some of her excitement, and smiled again. He said he hoped she didn't mind if they stopped for something to eat, and proceeded to drive for twenty minutes off the highway on wooded country roads to a place he knew. The waitress greeted him as "Mr. Alexander." He ordered a margarita. Isha had a glass of Chardonnay. She learned he'd studied medicine, although it took her a while to find out exactly what branch.

"Veterinarian?" she finally asked.

"Probably should have been. Probably more fun. No. Psychiatrist."

Isha laughed on cue but smelled danger, tried her best not to show it. Of all the things he could have been! She would have preferred him being a cop of some sort, more in her line of manageability. But a psychiatrist! Christ.

"Practicing?" she asked.

"Just three clients left. A fourth who calls once in a blue moon. Too many things I like to do. Boats, skiing. Can't let work get in the way."

Isha needed a minute to think. She excused herself to try her fiancé again. She picked a spot behind a half wall near the ladies' room, in Cameron's line of sight, and faked an agitated call, letting it go on for several minutes and raising her voice a couple of times before she hung up in obvious dismay.

Cameron said nothing when Isha returned to the table.

"Incredible," she said quietly, figuring it was past the time for hysterics. "I can't believe it. He's gone. Gone! Won't turn back, says he threw my bag into a dumpster at the next service area. Lucky I keep my jewelry with me." Cameron put his fork down, had a sip of his drink, and looked at her.

"Wow," he said.

Isha gave a little shrug, picked up her glass, and held it out. "Cheers," she said, with her most winning smile. "I seem to be on the used-girl market. Need a new girl-friend?"

Cameron clinked his glass with hers. "Best offer I've had today," he said with a grin.

They arrived in Larchmont in less than an hour. It was near 9:00 p.m., and on this cold winter Sunday night the Christmas lights were still on, but the sidewalks had been rolled up. Cameron drove through town and bore right around the head of the harbor, over a causeway leading to a sizable finger of land bearing a number of attractive homes, each of which was set on several landscaped acres of lawn. All of them had docks. There were lots of big trees. Cameron pulled into the driveway of one of the smaller houses, a handsome, two-story gray shingled house, and hit the button to open the door of a three-car garage. The light came on, revealing a silver Porsche 911, a Toyota pickup, kayaks hanging from the ceiling, oars leaning against the wall, and a variety of other gear for boats and fishing.

"I assume you are willing to stay here tonight," Cameron said before pulling into the garage. "It seems silly to go looking for a motel at this hour. I have plenty of room. If you don't mind. But if you do . . ."

"Thank you," Isha said. "You are very kind. I don't mind."

He pulled in, let Chum out, and grabbed his bag. Isha noted that he left the keys in the ignition.

Cameron gave her a quick tour. Living room, his study (off-limits except for patients), bathroom, mudroom, and kitchen. He pulled a bag of cookies out of a cabinet, offered them to her. She passed. He grabbed a couple of cookies and led the way upstairs.

"You can bunk here," he said. "My sister's room. She lives in Florida, leaves winter things here for her rare visits." Cameron looked at Isha's feet. "Her boots might fit you. You're about the same size. Bath is through here. You have a toothbrush in your bag? If not . . ."

"I have one."

"Good. Okay. Towels are in there. Shampoo, whatever. I'll be across the hall. But right now I'm going down to let Chum in, watch some football, and have a nightcap. Good game tonight. Pleased to have you join me."

"Do I get one question?"

"Let me guess. Am I married? No, not at the moment. And no, I'm not gay. Been married twice. Neither was terrible, just didn't work out. Not friends with either of them. Not enemies either. No kids. Maybe just not the marrying kind. Make yourself comfortable."

Listening to Cameron's footsteps descending the stairs, Isha was slightly dumbfounded. She walked over to the closet door, looked at herself in the full-length mirror. Nothing was out of place. She looked goddamn irresistible, as usual. The hair, the eyes, the bod — and this guy was going to watch football? She had to laugh, then realized she was laughing at herself. She did a little hip wiggle in front of the mirror, turned to the profile view that stretched her sweater oh so nicely, then collapsed on the bed. She had a shower, crawled underneath the puffy down quilt, and was soon asleep.

The smell of coffee and bacon woke her. She found sweatpants and a hoodie in the sister's things, some slippers, everything too big but manageable, and went downstairs. She tried unsuccessfully to sidestep Chum, who came over to greet her.

"Scrambled okay? Coffee. Juice in the fridge. Glasses up there. Toast on the table."

"Thank you."

"Now I get one question," Cameron said between

bites. "What's really going on?"

"What do you mean?"

"What I mean is that bit in the rest area, throwing your phone, the hysterics, the fantastic story about your fiancé abandoning you, leaving your bag in a dumpster, the sordid stuff about his awful family, and the amazing luck that you found me heading for Larchmont, which is where you needed to go . . ." Cameron was smiling. "The phone call at the restaurant was the topper. They don't have reception there yet. It's interesting. I like it. What's not to like about picking up this cool chick in the middle of a boring drive up the turnpike after a dull Christmas — at a rest area! This well-turned-out chick who whacks me with her phone and reels me in like a striper on an Atom popper, the whole thing like a late Christmas present you can't wait to open . . . and, okay, here we are having eggs and bacon and a delicious cup of java. I must say the company's good — usually it's just Chum and me, not that he's bad company — so I have to ask: What's really going on here . . . Nina?"

Isha took a sip of her coffee. She knew it. Goddamn psychiatrist. She made a quick decision. "Do you have room in your schedule to take me on as a patient?"

"Why would I do that?"

"Because then I would be protected. You have to take an oath, right? 'Hippo' or something like that."

Cameron laughed. "HIPAA."

"Whatever. Will you take me on?"

"I'm expensive."

"I always pay my debts."

"I imagine you do."

"Okay? Am I your patient Nina?"

"That will do. Yes. Okay. You are my patient Nina."

Nina put down her fork and got up from the table. She walked around to Cameron's chair and put her hand on the back of his neck. "Now would you like to open your late Christmas present?"

IV

TEST

It had been a pleasant ten days in Sydney. Andy and Becky had seen Grady every day, either at the boat during working hours or for drinks afterward, often followed by dinner. Pleasant, until one evening when Andy had been stunned to learn from Grady about his connection with a substantial drug deal that was imminent. That had been a curveball, finding out that his father was involved in something other than running and maintaining boats. Something illegal to boot. The information had rocked Andy. He'd just gotten rid of a revolting father figure who was a murderer. Now he found out his real father was running drugs? He was trying not to panic. But it was a nasty surprise. Andy supposed the drug deal had to do with boats, but he wasn't sure. Grady had let the cat out of the bag by accident one night after dinner. Becky hadn't been there, just Andy and Grady. A few drinks had loosened Grady's tongue. Afterward he was embarrassed, made it sound like nothing; made Andy swear he'd just forget it.

That was what Andy was trying to do, forget it, but finding himself immobilized in a fitness club that was closed for the night was making it difficult. Two hefty plainclothes cops had approached him as he'd left a marine-hardware shop late in the day. They said they needed him to answer a few questions having to do with The Race. They were insistent, said it would only take a minute, so he went with them to an office. Their IDs had looked legitimate. Suddenly they were asking questions about Grady, showing him photos of himself with Grady, photos of Grady with shady-looking characters they identified as persons of interest. Andy had played dumb. Sure, that's me and my father, so what? It had gotten tougher after that. They had shoved him around a bit, and started making threats. It turned out the "office" was part of a fitness club. The two men had taken Andy into the club and in a flash had slipped a line around his wrists and hauled him up until he was connected to the floor by his tiptoes.

The larger of the two men had slowly rolled up his sleeves as he approached Andy. The other had read him the riot act, how all they needed was information, how it didn't have to go this route, how he was going to tell them eventually, so he might as well spill it now — all the usual stuff out of a crime series. The big guy measured the distance to Andy's stomach, poked him with his fingers like he was testing a steak cooking on a grill, and clenched his fist. Andy was very frightened, stretched like he was, virtually hanging from his wrists, defenseless. One punch from this guy and he'd be broken. It was a terrifying feeling. Nothing to do. The good cop gave him one last chance to spill it. Desperate, Andy said, "Look, I can't tell you what I don't know. You want me to make something up?" The two cops nodded at one another. Bad cop cocked his fist. It was at that point that Grady appeared.

"Okay. Thanks, guys." Grady went to the cleat and lowered Andy. "Andy, meet Martin and Ted." The two shook hands with a very confused Andy and left the gym. Rubbing his wrists, Andy looked daggers at Grady.

"I had to know" was all Grady said, coiling the line and hanging it expertly on the cleat with a hitch.

They had driven to the boatyard in silence. Now they were sitting at a weather-beaten umbrella table in a private space near the water that went with Grady's digs. The lights from Harbour Bridge twinkled in the distance. They were sipping tequila, the good stuff, Don Julio 1942, and eating large shrimp dipped in a hot sauce. Andy was calming down as he listened to Grady tell him that the drug deal didn't exist, it was just a story he'd cooked up to test Andy. It wasn't his idea, the test, but he had to admit it made sense. His partners had insisted. They had pointed out that while Andy might be his son, he didn't really know him. They were right. A quick test seemed appropriate.

"Your partners?"

"You passed. But I need your assurance that what I tell you is in the vault. Can you do that, knowing that what happened in the gym, or worse, could actually happen without me showing up? The chances are remote, but it could . . . happen."

Andy stared at Grady.

"That's it. No blood oath. Just your assurance. That's how it works."

Andy got up from the table and walked to the yard's edge, where the light-flecked water was lapping at the rocky embankment. He didn't really know enough to make such a momentous decision, but he knew it was serious, this assurance he was being asked to pledge. The test had been scary. He'd surprised himself, faced with substantial physical damage — bad pain, lasting effects, damage that would have caused him to retire from The Race — by how he had kept his mouth shut. That had been either brave or stupid, frequent but always strange bedfellows. If someone had posed that situation and asked him what he would do, he probably would have said he would talk, spill the beans. But he hadn't. He hardly knew Grady, but he had protected him. His father. Blood on the tracks. It boiled down to trust, and trust was relatively new to Andy. For twenty-five years he had trusted only his mother, a broken woman. Then Becky had come back into his life, with love and trust wrapped in a gorgeous package. And now Grady. Was he being seduced by trust? He hoped not. He walked back to the table and sat down, looked Grady in the eyes.

"You have my assurance."

Grady reached in his inside jacket pocket and pulled out a one-inch stainless tube six inches long. It was capped at both ends. He handed it to Andy, who weighed it in his hands, pulled off the caps, held it up and looked through it at the bridge.

"So?"

"On a good day, that little can will hold around a million bucks or more in emeralds and opals."

Andy was still staring through the tube at the bridge. The lights were flickering like diamonds. His ears had to be deceiving him. Emeralds, opals, two of Australia's most plentiful stones, a million bucks' worth in a little stainless tube, what the hell . . . He looked at Grady, whose face had assumed that blank look he had mastered. Andy put the caps back on the tube, handed it to his father.

"That's why we had to test you. We've had this thing going nearly twenty years. It works because of the people involved. Normally a dicey game like this is regulated by violence, tough stuff. People get hurt, or, ultimately, disappeared if they get greedy. Drug-cartel stuff. That's not us. I've never been sure what holds us together. It's something pretty deep. Basic. I often go over it. The only thing we all have in common is security. By that I mean we're all well enough off. Not wealthy, but doing okay. Not desperate, anyway. All have a reasonably decent living doing whatever. Our group, our family, that's the right name for it, is about several things: trust, privilege, honor — old-time values. Pride too. And fun, oddly enough. It's fun, what we do. Exciting. Keeps our hearts started."

Andy poured himself a worthy shot of Don Julio. His imagination was running wild. He had a dozen questions, mostly details beginning with "How?"

Grady laughed. "What do you think?"

"How many are involved?"

"Maybe eight principal guys. Two at the mine, both high-end. That's the secret. High-end. Makes it easier to obtain the goods, know when to lay back. Our policy:

take no chances. Time means nothing. No such thing as deadlines. Recognizing opportunity is everything. Keeping within those guidelines — and we do — it could take us a couple years to fill up one of these little capsules.

"The lapidaire is next. Lapidarist, in English. He's the guy who does the cutting and grinding to see what's in those little clumps of dirt the mine sends him. Lapidary, that's his trade. The guy at the mine looks at a lump you can hold in the palm of your hand and sees a little green edge peeking out, thinks it has potential. The lapidaire does his work and says he's right or wrong. If he's right, how right? One carat, two, six? Now he's identified something they can sell. Did I say the lapidaire works for the mine? Because they don't have anything to sell until he confirms it. That's why the mine guys have to be high up. The lapidaire makes three.

"Then there's me, a couple mates at other yards catering to big boats, Martin and Ted — lower-level guys, hands-on, but they get a good share — and the wholesaler in New York. What's that, maybe seven or eight. Others are involved, middlemen, messengers, but they don't know it. When they deal with the wholesaler they don't care where the products come from."

"You said big boats?"

"Big enough. Don't have to be maxis. But yeah, fifty- to sixty-footers and up. Big enough to be going somewhere, like back to the States."

"Back to the States."

"That's the sales point. Our wholesaler is the best. Been in the business forever. Has lots of customers. His son works with him, a chip off the old block. They know how to handle the money, a little at a time here and there, which is great because it's always coming in."

"How does that work — electronic transfers? It must be as difficult to get the money out as it is to get the jewels in."

"Cash. All cash. One of us flies to the States every few months and brings back cash that can't be traced. A little at a time."

"You hide that little capsule on a boat going to the USA."

"Right," Grady said. "A boat like *All American*."

Andy had to laugh at that.

"That's what I mean by opportunity," Grady said. "There I am in Fremantle, minding my own business, knowing that after twenty-one months we have a full capsule just dying to travel, and there you are, suddenly, my own son, in the flesh, owner of a boat that's heading for Miami two legs from now. Talk about timing, talk about opportunity . . ."

Andy had stopped laughing.

V

PLAN B

Isha, Chum the Labrador, and Cameron were in his twenty-six-foot RIB (rubber inflatable), cruising across the deserted Larchmont harbor full of winter sticks used as mooring keepers. She'd thought it was strange of him to suggest going on the water in December, with the temperature in the low forties and the wind gusting, but the Protector runabout's custom pilothouse was tight and also heated. It was comfortable. Cameron said he enjoyed using the boat all winter.

Isha had been desperately crafting her story from the moment Cameron had told her he was a psychiatrist. She didn't have it quite worked out, but she knew it had to have a fairly solid foundation of reality. She figured a psychiatrist was fed a steady diet of bullshit from his patients. He'd have heard it all, and could surely spot fabrication from a hundred miles away in the fog. What she'd told him about her supposed boyfriend's fractured family was right out of her own background, if a tad sugarcoated, so she could leave that in place. She wasn't quite sure about the rest. Did this Hippo thing really work? Would Cameron call the cops if he knew she was on the lam? The accessory-to-murder bit was off-limits, for sure. Plus they'd have to prove that. She had to come up with where she was going, what she needed to do. But first she needed to learn more about Cameron. Where better than in bed?

The way Cameron had opened his late Christmas present was extremely and pleasantly telling. He wasn't one of those guys who just tore off the paper and pulled open the box. Far from it. He took his time, relishing every moment. He showed appreciation for the attractive wrapping, removed the bow with care, peeled back the scotch tape and removed the paper gently, like he was saving it for next year. He handled the package with curiosity, his hands discovering clues, and when he finally opened it, his delight was heartfelt, exciting, and prolonged. So was Isha's. She was quite overcome, in fact, suddenly finding herself out there in the stratosphere, suspended in a powerful fantasy realm of sensations where she had rarely ever been. Tears of joy had dampened her face. When she woke up, Cameron was dozing next to her. Chum had come in and put a paw on him. He woke up. In a conversational tone, he explained to Chum that his breakfast was going to be delayed. Chum groaned and lay down beside the bed while his master revisited his present, this time more directly, but with the same measured intensity. Once more Isha was transported. She cursed herself for letting this man have the upper hand. That was her trick. But her curse was empty, and she knew it.

As Cameron drove the Protector at slow speed, describing the harbor, throwing in a bit of history along with weather information and pointing out landmarks of interest, Isha half listened. She remained distracted by the events of the morning that were still vibrating. She had started talking in bed, but Cameron had made her get up, put on a robe, and have a seat in his office. "You're my patient now; let's do it right," he had told her.

"You don't usually bed your patients?"

"Only the ones I pick up at rest areas," he said with a smile.

She had to admit the office was a good idea. Professional. Hippo would be in place. She talked. She admitted she had gone to the rest area to find a ride into Larchmont, where she was looking for someone; that she had picked Cameron out based on his late-model car and the sticker on the back window. "I liked the look of you, too," she had added.

"How flattering," he said, "to be selected out of the crowd at the Vince Lombardi rest area."

"My plan," she said, "was to distract you with sex after a couple drinks, then steal your car while you were sleeping."

"What a devil you are."

"Why didn't that work?" Isha put on a frown.

"Because I didn't show any interest. Although I admit it was difficult. You are a very tempting package. But using football and Chum was a good way to distract you. It was obvious that bringing you in here was risky. No idea exactly why, but that didn't matter. I felt secure in my bed. Chum sleeps in my room. He's a light sleeper and hates to be startled. There's a trick to opening the garage door. And frankly, I've been bored of late. When you heaved your phone at me, I thought, Okay, here we go. But let's back up. What got you to Vince Lombardi?"

"A bus."

Isha told him that what she'd said about her supposed fiancé's family was really about her family, only in truth it was a lot worse. Against her better judgment, she'd made the mistake of visiting them on Christmas; they lived in the Bronx, and it had been a nightmare. It had been several years since she'd seen them. Her mother had advanced to a very ugly stage of alcoholism. The house was a shambles, and her stepfather had attacked her while she slept. She'd fought him off successfully because he too had been drinking all day. She told Cameron she'd hit him with a ten-pound weight she'd been able to grab from under the bed. She hoped he wasn't dead, or maybe she hoped he was dead. In any case she'd quickly dressed, grabbed her bags, and taken their car to a motel. The next morning she'd returned the car to a strip mall near their house and had a taxi take her to the Port Authority in Manhattan, where she put her suitcase in a locker before boarding a bus to the Vince Lombardi.

Cameron was good. He let "Nina" talk without much feedback. He found himself pleasantly stimulated by this new patient. He could sense there was a better-than-average story to be discovered here, maybe some real dynamite, and he looked forward to hearing it fleshed out. And speaking of flesh, man, what a delightful bonus.

This could be just what Cameron needed. He had been practicing nearly thirty years, and he was burned out, sick of it, sick of the sickness that permeated the human condition. There wasn't anyone alive who wasn't a little crazy. Earth was definitely the asylum for the universe, as Einstein had noted. Cameron wasn't so sure about the $C=MC^2$ business, but the great mathematician had sure nailed the asylum bit. Cameron was convinced that to be human you had to be crazy. It was just a question of how crazy, and what temperament. At least half of Cameron's patients had been self-defined lunatics, eating out on therapy because they could afford his ridiculous rates. It was something to do. Over cocktails his patients loved quoting a line here and there from "my shrink." It seemed to give them status, like owning a fancy sports car, or a racehorse.

Cameron had started out on the right foot, thinking he could help his fellow man, duly responding to his wealthy father's "need to give back" obsession. He'd gone to the right schools, studied under the best people, graduated well, hung out his shingle, then sat and listened to the sad, twisted stories and prescribed the various drugs until he wanted to tear his hair out. He'd helped a few people along the line. He knew that. The rest either were beyond help or, frankly, didn't need it. They just enjoyed the prescriptions. And the attention. Along the way he'd gotten a bit of a reputation for, as Nina or whatever the hell her name was had said, bedding his female patients. It was strictly against the rules, and there had been a couple of close calls, but it had worked out. Getting naked was what psychiatry was all about, after all. Call it research.

Dr. Cameron did finally ask why Larchmont had been Nina's destination. She'd told him she was looking for a certain person who could help her locate some people she needed to find, people who had cheated her. "Ah," he said, "sounds like a revenge mission, always perilous."

"But oh so satisfying," Nina said, looking daggers.

Cameron had just nodded. He'd tried it a few times, if truth be told, and Nina had a point: it was satisfying if it didn't blow up in your face. "Does this person you're looking for have a name? Since I'm a local, I just might know him."

Isha hesitated. She was playing it by ear. She didn't have a master plan yet. She thought becoming his patient had been smart, but how far to go was still in question. Putting a name out there seemed risky. She was okay with this guy, this psychiatrist who appeared to be a player. But did she trust him — at all? She'd been studying the displays in his office, which were obviously selected to calm and cajole, to inspire exactly the kind of trust she was thinking about. Or at least to inspire confidence that the fellow you were exposing your soul to was cool, sensitive enough to handle it with care. There were his various professional certificates and academic degrees, but more telling were the photos of Cameron fly-fishing in some picturesque mountain stream; Cameron at the helm of a large sailboat; Cameron and Chum strolling in a sun-dappled wood. The few paintings were originals by name artists, gorgeous landscapes full of hypnotic light and subdued color.

Trust was not a condition Isha was familiar with. Trust had never been a factor in her fraudulent life, unless she played it as a joker to gain an advantage. She knew nothing could get you busted quicker than trust. Trust for her was the resort of fools, a crutch of the weak, and here she was, actually contemplating it. What the hell! But everything had to be reevaluated at this juncture. She was breaking new ground, meaning new tactics had to be considered. Well-considered chances taken. And this Cameron was a very smart dude. He actually felt safe to her, in the short term anyway. She was already out on this limb, and while he had the saw, there was no sign of him even contemplating picking it up. He almost felt like a fellow conspirator. Almost. In a supporting role.

"Roger Davis," Isha said. RD, the guy Mitchell had put inside the All American syndicate, on the boat, and whom he had paid handsomely to mess with Andy. RD, who had made Andy look like a fool on the Outward Bound boulder course when he pulled away the knotted rope Andy was making the leap of faith to grab; RD, who had surely unclipped Andy's safety belt that night when they were working to subdue a torn, flailing jib on the foredeck of *All American* in mid-ocean during a gale. If another crewman hadn't tackled Andy on the way by, he would have been washed overboard and drowned. RD, whom Andy had shoved over the side and subsequently fired at the dock in Fremantle, Western Australia, in front of the whole crew, after Mitchell — and Isha — had been busted and Andy had assumed ownership of the boat. These were events Isha hadn't known about until after the fact. They were events Mitchell had planned in his childish hang-up to denigrate Andy whenever possible. Or kill him.

But Isha had found out about them, and figured RD was just the person she needed to help wreak her revenge on Andy, and on his bitchy girlfriend who had ruined her getaway attempt. RD had been burned, humiliated by Andy — maybe rightfully, but no matter. RD had to want revenge as much as she did. And Mitchell had proved RD could be had. Isha figured she could mold RD into an excellent associate. She had his name and particulars in a crew file she'd found on a disc she'd taken from the apartment. Fifteen or twenty phone calls later, and she'd located him somewhere in the Larchmont area. Rumor had it he had taken a job on a sizable sailing vessel. Made sense. That was what he knew.

Cameron said he didn't know RD, but he suggested they take the RIB, make a few stops at boatyards and marinas and check out the scuttlebutt. Plus it was a nice day for a cruise.

"Who will I be?" Isha asked.

"Who would you like to be?" Cameron asked. "A woman I picked up at a rest area? A new patient? Don't worry. The guys are used to seeing me with women. Just be Nina."

VI

DRILLING

"Evening, Mr. Moss," the security guard said. His name tag read Darryl Cronin. "'S late."

"'Lo, Darryl. It is. Couldn't sleep. Had to check a couple things that are keeping me up."

"Yes sir. Go right ahead."

"I'll be on the boat for at least an hour. Take a break if you want. Get yourself a snack."

"You mean it, sir?"

"I do. Just give me a whistle when you're back."

"Could use a bite. Thanks."

"I'll try not to shoot anyone," Andy said. Darryl laughed.

Andy had made sure the hard area where most of the boats were parked was deserted. He'd arranged to have *All American* launched late that afternoon for an early-morning sail to test a new jib. It was moored at the furthest dock out. The first thing he did was flip the running lights on and off three times. The boat was moored bow out. The red port light was blocked by the wall of the dock. The green starboard light could only be seen by someone off-shore who was watching. Then he removed the cabin sole boards. He didn't have to wait long before he felt someone step aboard. Damned if it wasn't Martin, the guy who had been ready to break his ribs when he'd been hauled up by the wrists in the gym. Martin, the size of a tight end. Andy knew Martin had come by boat, but he hadn't heard a sound. He had a large duffel bag with him, which he handed down the hatch to Andy. The bag nearly knocked Andy over. It must have weighed fifty pounds or more.

"Juice?" Martin asked, after the briefest nod of recognition.

"Plugged in," Andy said, feeling slightly uncomfortable.

Martin wasn't a talker. First he pulled the hatch shut. He got right to work exposing the keel bolts. He knew exactly what to do. Andy later found out that construction plans hadn't been that difficult to get if you knew the right people. For Martin, a boat builder and mechanic, it was a piece of cake. Andy could only watch nervously as Martin, wearing a dull headlamp, took out a Dremel tool and quickly ground through the tack weld on the aftermost starboard bolt of five pairs. Using a long wrench, and with considerable effort, he unscrewed it. It was a five-eighths-by-six-inch threaded bolt that went through an aluminum floor plate atop several inches of fiberglass into a tapped hole in the thick flange of the steel fin that supported the bulb, twelve feet down. There was a heavy lock washer at the top. Andy knew half the bolts were redundant, but still, messing with keel bolts gave him a twinge.

Andy had another twinge when Martin began removing the companion bolt. Martin felt Andy's tension and stopped. "Relax," he said quietly, "and watch." After cutting the weld and unscrewing the second bolt, Martin pulled a small piece of three-eighths steel plate out of his bag. It measured around twelve inches by four inches, Andy figured. It had two holes drilled in it. Martin laid the plate down, matched the hole on the floor with one hole in the plate, replaced the second bolt he had removed, and snugged it tight. The other hole, Andy noted with amazement, matched the hole where the first bolt had been removed. He was impressed.

Martin pulled a portable magnetic drill press out of the duffel. No wonder the bag had been so heavy. He set the robust unit on the steel plate and handed Andy the cord. Andy plugged it into a nearby socket. "What I'm gonna do is widen the hole a half inch with this drill, and make the hole a quarter inch deeper," Martin said. "I flip this switch here, and this beauty magnets to the steel plate I just secured. The hole in the plate is a guide. This thing is loud. Take this." He pulled a folded, heavy sound-absorption blanket out of his bag. "Cover me." With that, Martin bent to the task, got the drill lined up, and nodded to Andy. Andy covered him. "Okay?" Martin's query was muffled.

"Okay," Andy said. Martin started the drill.

Andy was amazed at how much the sound was muffled. He knew it could be heard underwater, but that seemed safe enough at 2:00 a.m. In eight minutes that seemed like an hour, Martin was done. He turned off the drill and flung the sound sheet off him. His face was sheened with sweat. Anyone with less strength than Martin would have had a hard time handling the magnetic drill and lining it up. He put the drill it back in the bag, removed the steel plate, and replaced the second bolt. He gathered the drill curls and dumped them in the bag. He pulled out a little electric vacuum and sucked up the powdery stuff. With a rag he wiped up the oil residue. He pulled out a plastic tackle box and removed the top of a bolt and regular washer that exactly matched the top of the bolt he'd removed.

In another box was the stainless tube, which had been sealed. He held it up and stared at it, then handed it to Andy. A million bucks in his hands. Martin stared at him. Andy passed his open hand slowly over the top of the capsule and handed it back to Martin, who gave an approving nod. Martin dropped the capsule into the hole he'd just drilled. It fit perfectly. He set the bolt top and washer over the hole. It matched the other bolts perfectly. Nothing looked amiss.

"How do you seal it?" Andy asked quietly.

Martin's smile was wry. "With polyurethane glue." He chuckled quietly. "And a drop of solder that looks just like a tack weld," Martin said, removing a small soldering gun from his bag.

"Yo, Mr. Moss!"

Andy and Martin froze. It was the security guard. Andy grabbed his mobile phone and snapped it to his ear as he flung open the hatch.

"Hey, Darryl, okay, just on the phone right now. I'll

be finishing up. Catch you on my way out. All quiet."

"Yes sir, okay."

Andy and Martin sat in silence for a good five minutes to make sure Darryl had returned to the gate. Then Martin glued the bolt top over the hole, laid drops of solder over the old tack welds, put the floor back together, and packed up while Andy made sure nothing was out of place.

"Go to the gatehouse, keep him busy," Martin said as he prepared to leave. "My RIB's all electric, but still . . ."

"One thing."

Martin stopped.

"Would you really have hit me?"

Martin picked up the duffel like it was a bag of feathers. "Naw," he said with a smile that could have gone either way, and disappeared up the hatch.

VII

RD

"I never unclipped him. Nobody could prove that. I did not unclip him."

"Mitch said you did, and that he paid you plenty."

"Mitch is full of it."

"I know what I know. What about the business on the boulders, when you pulled away the rope Andy was trying to grab. I saw it. I watched the video."

"Kid stuff. Just harassing the boss's son. He had a safety line. What's all this anyway? What do you want? How in hell did you find me?"

Roger Davis, better known as RD, and Isha were sitting below in the varnished mahogany, teak, and holly tufted leather elegance of a classic seventy-foot wooden yawl designed by Sparkman & Stephens and built in the late 1930s. It had been fully renovated and upgraded with an electric heating system that was on against the December chill, maintaining a comfortable temperature of sixty-eight degrees. The encounter, however, was not comfortable.

Isha had figured it wouldn't be, and that was just fine. She'd picked RD for many reasons. The fact that he was in the sailing business and had an inside track for what happened on the grand-prix circuit was one. The fact that Andy had humiliated RD in front of the crew was another, because it was a humiliation that would dog his career. Mitch's files on the disc she'd taken from the safe the night of the arrest had proof of payments and incriminating emails that would put RD away if she chose to use them. But the main reason was that Mitch had selected RD for the down-and-dirty end of things, the elimination of Andy, and he'd come through. RD had done his thing. It was just his bad luck that one of the crew had been perfectly positioned to tackle Andy as he went streaming by on a load of water during that frightening night in the middle of nowhere. Isha had gathered all the details. Mitch had whined about his bad luck often enough.

Isha also figured RD could be manipulated as long as there was money involved. And sex. She'd heard he liked to brag about his supposed success with women. That would be an easy card for her to play. But mainly it was the revenge factor. She knew how strong that motivation was for her. The satisfaction revenge provided was one of those IMAX-quality productions, with full-range, wraparound, body-vibrating stereo sound and high-resolution, 5D laser-video production that left one weak with gratification. Was it corrosive? Was it permanently damaging to one's benevolent instincts because of all the vile planning and mean-spirited energy it took to execute? No doubt. Cameron knew. He'd talked with his patient Nina about revenge, admitted he'd dabbled in it a few times, and mused about the toll it could take, the perversion it required; how in its most compulsive stages it was an addiction. Cameron said he'd come to believe revenge should be considered the eighth deadly sin.

Isha knew he was right, knew she was addicted, knew there was nothing to do about it. Knew there was nothing she wanted to do about it. She didn't want patient Nina treated for it, and her good luck was that Cameron didn't seem to be interested in applying such treatment. Like any junkie, Isha craved the debilitating stereo sound and the blinding, high-resolution video that would send her into a sublime, manic dimension.

Isha knew RD was her guy. He had the right portfolio, the right goods — the right bads. He would be putty in her hands. She was supremely confident in her task, loaded to the brim like any good salesman with the glories of her product, ready to take on an entire congregation of peace-and-forgiveness freaks and turn them into vengeful connivers.

Once she'd identified RD as her mark, it hadn't been that difficult to find him. From Mitch's file she learned he'd worked the upper East Coast. Sailing pros tend to work a territory. She'd started making inquiries in sailing's capital, Newport, Rhode Island, then branched out to high-end, East Coast yacht havens in Greater Boston, Cape Cod, Stonington, Connecticut, and Blue Hill, Maine, until she'd hit pay dirt on Long Island Sound.

Running into Cameron had been a stroke of luck so far. At the third place they had stopped that day in his RIB, an older marina crony Cameron knew had said, "Yeah, pretty sure that's who Mark Creighton just hired as his skipper. Too bad old Barny Walton died, he'd run *Orion* for damn near forty years. You should see her. Just had a refit. Cost a fortune. Damn ole girl looks like new. Built in the thirties, you know. Just relaunched her. She's at Creighton's dock, Cormorant Cove, other side of Greenwich. Heard they're planning to send her south this winter. Creighton and Miss Nancy will fly, too old for that sort of passage. Yeah, heard the new guy just got off the Round the World Race. Heard he got flu or something. Haven't met 'im."

The next day Isha called and made an appointment to see RD, saying she was Nina Simpson and that she specialized in insurance for classic yachts. Cameron's idea. When she told Cameron, he'd tossed her the keys to the Porsche, saying it would help her make a good first impression. "Don't forget to take your shoes off," Cameron told her.

First she'd stopped at a local hair salon, where she had an appointment to have her hair rebleached. It didn't really need it, but Isha knew the best place to go for information about any town was the beauty parlor. The dropping of the Creighton name opened the floodgates. When she left, freshly blonde, Isha knew everything from the Creightons' daughter's arrest for shoplifting to ribald tales of the family's new boat captain, who called himself RD. One of the stylists had dated him. When queried, she shrugged. "I'd give him a six," she said, which had gotten a big laugh.

Isha found the Creightons' estate, stopped at the gatehouse, where RD had left her name, and followed the road around to the waterfront, where *Orion* was docked next to a handsome workshop. RD had certainly scored himself a gig, she thought as she took in the grandeur of the place, with every bush and tree guarding the gorgeous stone mansion trimmed and mulched to perfection. The gardens were properly winterized. She'd done some research on Creighton. He'd made his billions in fossil fuel. She'd placed her boots next to those presumably belonging to RD before she set foot on *Orion*'s spotless teak deck, and soon she was facing a slightly irate RD, a state that well suited her pitch.

RD had known Isha from a distance. He'd assumed she was Andy's eye candy until he'd been approached by Mitch. After that he'd figured out she was Mitch's pawn, and also his bedmate. Hands off, in other words. Along with the other guys in the crew, RD had thoroughly enjoyed watching Isha do her dances and work her various charms at syndicate events. Everyone agreed she was a dangerous piece of work, a climber, a femme fatale. Only RD had known her real priorities, which made watching her even more fun. They had never even been introduced.

But now . . . He'd heard about Mitch's arrest, and had lain low in case Mitch had decided to throw him under the bus. Having Andy knock him off the boat in Fremantle had been humiliating for sure, but it sure beat being arrested. That could have gotten ugly. He got to swim away from all that, literally. And landing the job on *Orion* provided great cover, not to mention a decent check every month. But now here came sexy little Isha calling on him, how about that, with some twisted little plan up her sleeve, no doubt. If Mitch had gotten busted, RD wondered, how had Isha slipped away, apparently free as a bird? Watch out! he cautioned himself, but for RD the sudden, even remote possibility of climbing into bed with one of the hottest women he'd ever laid eyes on took a certain amount of the edge off caution. RD's folly was well embedded.

"I'm sure you have many questions," Isha said. "Let me make it simple. I'm looking for an associate, that's what I want. I will let you in on a little secret. Andy Moss and that sweet little girlfriend of his have thrown a monkey wrench into my life. It has made me very angry. I want some payback. I thought you might be interested."

RD looked at his watch, then looked at her. "Isha," he said, "how 'bout we have a drink?"

"It's Nina," Isha said.

VIII

THE TASMAN

Two and a half days out of Sydney, skipper Jan Sargent and navigator Peter Damaris, who had been watching the weather faxes, let the crew of *All American* know that the Low they had been tracking was just hours away. Everything had been working well so far. The charts issued by the Australian Bureau of Meteorology, based on data from sea buoys, had helped them negotiate the tricky current that runs south to north off Sydney. Like a mini Gulf Stream, the current is laced with many a strong eddy. The piping northwesterly had come in on schedule, giving them a twenty-five-knot push in the right direction. On a beam reach, they'd been averaging eighteen knots, with gusts frequently pushing them over twenty-five. There had been some debate over setting the spinnaker, but with the wind angle barely more than ninety degrees, Sargent was adamant about leaving the sail in the bag. "Maybe it would give us another knot or two," he told his crew, "until either we crashed and burned or we blew it out. To win, it helps to finish."

The leg from Sydney to Auckland around the top of New Zealand isn't that long — around 1,400 miles as a boat sails (1,200 miles measured in straight lines) — but it is one of those tricky passages you wouldn't want to do for pleasure with your family. For a race boat it takes about five days. One sails out of Sydney into the Tasman Sea until off Cape Reinga, at the north end of New Zealand, where the Pacific Ocean is waiting. Sailors often refer to the Tasman as a bad part of the world. Boats have been lost there.

"New Zealand is so small it doesn't affect the weather like Australia does," Grady had told Andy a few days before the start. "Little New Zealand is parked in the weather motorway. The wind just whizzes over the top." Luckily for Andy, Grady had sailed Sydney to Auckland a number of times. "You can't cross the Tasman without going through at least one big front," Grady had told him. "The Highs come across the Great Australian Bight into the Tasman, giving you that nice nor'wester. The Lows come from the Southern Ocean, and they're strong, bringing with them a forty-to-fifty-degree wind shift that's also in the twenty-five-to-thirty-knot range. You can end up sailing through a succession of fronts and ridges. Big fun."

Andy was driving, and loving it. It was night. The number three jib was slightly high cut, meaning it wasn't constantly filling with water and pulling the nose down. Despite its lack of buoyancy forward, *All American* was behaving quite well. Spray was constant, but the bow was staying clean most of the time. The helmsman was partly responsible for that, driving the boat off a few degrees in the gusts, and accelerating to boot. Andy had a friendly star he kept lined up on the forestay as a safe course. He worked the boat up in the lighter spots to come closer to the heading for Cape Reinga. Head trimmer Dave Zimmer, with Larry Kolegeri, the former New York Jets linebacker, on the handles, were minding the main, working with Andy, easing in the gusts to decrease helm pressure, and trimming back constantly. EMT Joe Dugan and Dick Hooper, who had replaced the dismissed Roger Davis, were doing the same with the jib.

For Andy, once into the rhythm of it, the pleasure, the satisfaction, was immense. It was like steering a high-performance dinghy, a 470, or a Melges, only frighteningly more impressive when *All American* planed down a wave and all sixty feet of it was so in tune with wind and water that it felt suspended in time and space — steady as a rock, locked into a slender groove — with the speedo climbing to twenty-three, twenty-five, twenty-seven; with helm, boat, and sails seeming frozen for as much as five or eight seconds (a forever moment), pushing through the reality of that tenuous envelope of performance the designer had glimpsed in his dreams.

As all-consuming as it was for the helmsman, because the satisfaction involved was conducive, thoughts of Becky came rushing in as fast as the water was streaking past. Physical stuff first to accompany the rush Andy felt driving this race boat in full fly, swaddled in foul-weather gear, with every muscle working to stay upright on the slippery, pitching platform, with water running down his neck and spray blocking his vision. His hands were trying to stay light on the wheel for best communication with the powerful beast. And there came the vision of Becky beside him, naked, the two of them entwined, laughing, crying out. But it was a trick, his mind letting her in like that, because the last meetings with her had been a little tense.

He'd struggled about telling her of the deal he'd made with his father, about the small container worth a million or more in emeralds and opals that was now buried in *All American*'s keel. That was what Grady had wanted to know. "Will you tell Becky?" he'd asked. Grady said experience had taught him that if a person is told a secret, they will always tell one person. He wanted to know: Would that one person be Becky? He went on to say he rather hoped it would be. Because maybe Andy could make it end there, create such a dire potential consequence that Becky would break the rule and her lips would actually be sealed. Andy said he'd let Grady know. Before he boarded the boat for the Auckland leg, Andy had taken his father aside and said yes, he had told Becky.

Not telling her would have been impossible, because she would know something was amiss. Her antennae were that sensitive. But he hadn't imagined how difficult telling her would be. Photography had kept her busy in Sydney. The advertising department back home at Moss Optics was delighted with the material she'd been sending them. And thanks to a woman she'd met, a friend of Grady's who was a climate-change activist, she'd become captivated by that subject. Bill McKibben's frightening book *The End of Nature* had just come out, in 1989, and it had become the environmental activists' bible, even in Sydney. McKibben had written about — documented! — the rapid increase of carbon dioxide in the atmosphere and had gone deeply into the sobering specifics of the crippling damage warming of the planet would cause; how there were already ominous signs of regression. In 1988, for the first time in history, Americans had eaten more food than their country grew. In the last ten years acid rain had become ten to forty times more toxic. There were a couple of hundred pages of similarly disturbing facts.

Becky had attended a few climate meetings in Sydney that at first glance had seemed to Andy like a bunch of alarmists wringing their hands over another vague threat that was far in the future. As Jan Sargent had put it: "Yeah, we're all gonna die someday, so what." McKibben's point was that unless some very radical stance was taken immediately, the "end of nature" could or would happen sooner than one might imagine. Few had the time, or the fortitude, to even contemplate such immense, terminal disruption. Denial ruled, as usual, and life lurched on. Except Becky, the lawyer, had taken it on as a personal case. Her research file was growing at a rapid rate. Andy was finding it difficult to get her attention on occasion. Evenings when there was no Race-related social event, she would be buried in research, often stopping to read key passages to him from texts she had found. He began to get interested.

His wrists had caught her attention. They had taken a chafing from being hauled up onto his tiptoes at the fitness gym while being "tested." When Becky had inquired, Andy had made up a tale of how he'd wrapped lines around both wrists to help haul a heavy sail onto the dock. She'd bought it, he'd thought. But a couple of days later they were lying in bed enjoying the afterglow when she had said quietly, while stroking his wrist, "Why don't you tell me what really happened."

Andy didn't say anything. Neither did Becky. When the silence started to get just a touch awkward, Andy said, "Okay . . . a couple rough dudes grabbed me and before I knew it they had hauled me up onto my tiptoes and threatened to do damage if I didn't tell them about Grady's drug deal."

Becky enjoyed a good laugh. "I knew it had to be something like that," she'd said, giving Andy a hug, enjoying his joke. Andy didn't laugh, and he didn't hug back. It took a minute, but Becky slowly sat up in bed, looking curiously at Andy like she might be observing a new client she was meant to defend.

"You're not kidding," she said.

"I'm not kidding."

Becky had fallen back on the bed with her eyes closed while Andy had told her everything, from Grady's rendition of why this casual smuggling operation had worked for such a long time to the details of how Martin, the same guy who had helped string him up, had expertly drilled into the lead keel, sealed the canister in with polyurethane glue, and silently slipped away into the night on his electric-powered RIB. "If you love me, if you want me to stay healthy, this information must stay between us," Andy had said in conclusion.

There had been a pause so long that Andy had dozed off.

"How could you?" Becky said it quietly, but it stirred him.

"How could I not?" he mumbled.

"They could put you away for a long time. I guess you've thought about that. And what it would do to Moss Optics. My God, Sam! It would kill him."

"Here's the thing," Andy said. "I don't know about it. Someone snuck onto the boat and buried the canister in the keel. And of course I'm not taking any money. There's nothing to trace. I have thought about it."

Becky went quiet. Andy remembered her getting up and walking to the bathroom, always a pleasing sight, and closing the door. He also remembered thinking, What have I done? A minute later she had opened the door and stuck her head out. "I hate that Grady used you," she'd said, "but my lips are sealed."

"WAVE!!"

It was Stu Samuels. Andy had sensed it a touch too late. SLAM! The bow plunged into the middle of it, scooping up a Niagara of water that rolled down the weather deck like a little tsunami and tried its best to tear Andy and the sailors in the cockpit away from their safety harnesses. It took a while for everyone to recover and take stock of their personal discomfort, because the best foul-weather gear was no match for such a hosing. Everyone was soaked to the skin. The cockpit was full, taking its time to drain. Larry Kolegeri was the first to find his voice. "Becky. Right, boss?"

Andy: "Becky."

"Worth it?" It was Stu.

"Not for you guys," Andy said, laughing. The boys

joined in, spicing their laughter with obscenities.

Pete Damaris, the navigator, stuck his head out the hatch. "If you're through having water fights, we have to get serious about this new front. It's about on us, and it's boisterous. Southwest at twenty-five to thirty. A ninety-degree shift. What you been steering?"

"Oh-six-five, average."

"Good."

Jan Sargent came up behind Peter. "Jibe, change jibs after if we have to."

"If the Low is that close," Andy said, "why don't we jibe now before we're in the mess of two systems colliding, with confused wind and seas. We'll be off course for a few minutes, but it might be a lot easier to be on the right jibe when the front hits."

"The sooner we jibe the better angle we'll have on the new tack," Peter said.

"Do it," Jan said. "Want help?"

"We're good."

"Okay below."

"Ready to jibe, guys," Andy said as he began steering down. It was going to be tricky. The nor'wester had been blowing for several days, building the seas to what looked like twenty feet. Andy put the boat on a more comfortable broad reach and kept looking off the port quarter for a smooth patch in which to jibe. He noted boat speed was under fifteen knots. There it was: the flat spot he'd been looking for.

"Now!" he yelled, and turned the wheel, going for slow but steady, knowing control was everything to keep this wild-ass thoroughbred from taking charge. The boat speed helped, reducing the apparent wind speed to ten or fifteen knots, but boat speed was dropping. Oncoming seas from astern looked menacing. Zimmer handled the main beautifully, trimming as much as he could as the force came off it for a couple of seconds, then easing big time on the new tack. Even with gloves and turns on the winch drum, the heat of the wet line running through his hands was uncomfortably hot. Trim and get speed up and they'd be good.

"JAM!" Dugan yelled. "Got a jam."

Andy had already started to come up a few degrees to avoid accidentally jibing back, an event that could cause serious damage. But the jib was now backwinded by the jammed weather sheet, which was bent taut around the mast, awkwardly filling the jib and pulling the bow down. Andy fought it, thinking if he could block the jib, if he could put the main between it and the wind, it might release enough pressure for Dugan and Hooper to clear the jam. He allowed the boat to head down a few perilous degrees, hoping the waves would give him the break he needed. When he felt the stern rising up under him he said goodbye to any break, thank you very much. The wave from behind lifted the stern and drove the boat forward. Andy hung on as he watched the bow dive like an arrow dropped from the sky into the back of the next wave and keep going, playing submarine, with green water rushing up past the forward hatch until it was at the base of the mast, stopping the yacht dead at a steep angle that revealed the entire rudder. The boat hung there for the longest second ever measured until it simply fell over on its side. At some point in the nightmare Andy was sure he heard Joe Dugan yell, "Clear!"

The spreaders pierced the water before the mast slowly began to stand upright again. Good old Dugan and Hooper had scrambled to the new leeward side as soon as it was available and had begun trimming the now released jib on the proper side. It was just what was needed, as the jib pulled the boat away from the wind and provided some momentum. Andy felt the rudder, immersed again, take hold. Zimmer let the main remain eased as things returned to normal, as water cascaded off the deck back to where it belonged.

Jan Sargent's face appeared in the cockpit hatch. He looked like he'd been keelhauled. "That's a radical way to clear a jammed jib sheet," Sargent said.

"I'll write it up for the sailors' handbook," Andy said.

Forty minutes later the Low came through, snarling and gnashing its teeth with great cracks of lightning and echoing, rolling thunder so loud it was alarming. It was raining hard, and blowing twenty-five as predicted. The seas were a tangled mess as the southwest wind arm-wrestled with the northerly. Everyone had had a chance to go below and re-dress in dry clothes before putting their wet foulies back on, a marked improvement. Speed remained over twenty knots, and the sou'wester was making it comfortable to steer a course of eighty degrees. They were on a reach for Cape Reinga. Stu Samuels was driving.

As dawn broke and the sou'wester had abated somewhat, producing a more reliable seaway, Sargent called for one of the smaller, tougher spinnakers. Soon they were flying, rarely under twenty-five knots, and under control as they planed down wave after wave. It was one of those unforgettable moments under sail as the sun rose over the bow, backlighting the wild-looking pathway of breaking seas in front of them and brightening their wake: pronounced streaks of white foam in a tight V that looked like someone should be waterskiing behind them. No one talked. Even Sargent was impressed.

The following morning the sunrise showed them the light on Cape Reinga, with famous Ninety Mile Beach to the right. "You know that beach is really fifty-five miles," Teddy Bosworth said. "More Kiwi bullshit."

They'd changed to the largest spinnaker, and the speed was diminishing as they outraced the Low into the more moderate southwest sea breeze along New Zealand's west coast. Indications were that even lighter winds could be expected. They had lost track of their rival, *Ram Bunctious*, in what was most definitely turning out to be a two-boat race. Damaris said he thought *Ram* had gone further to the north. A few hours later, his suspicions were proved right as the Kiwis were spotted. *Ram* looked to be a few miles ahead, and at least two miles north of Cape Reinga.

"We are where we are," Sargent said. "We'll go for the beach."

"I like it," Andy said, recalling what Grady had told him about the little sea breeze that could often be found off Cape Reinga. The sun was a promising sign. If Koonce on *Ram Bunctious* was sensing the same thing, it was too late. He was too far offshore to come in. He'd made his choice. Too late to change his mind. The water was deep within a half mile of the beach. In the light wind that had come northwest, *All American* had jibed spinnaker and slid around Cape Reinga and North Cape to the east. They watched *Ram* sail into a hole outside and end up a mile behind them.

Another jibe and *All American* turned south into the typical northeast sea breeze on the east coast that would take them the two hundred fifty miles to the finish in Auckland. With *Ram* visible but well behind them, there was a certain quiet comfort on board *All American*. The wind was blowing a steady ten knots. The big reaching chute was doing its job. The off watch was topside, taking the sun.

Below, Damaris, Sargent, and Andy were not sharing that comfort as they looked ahead and struggled with their final strategic decision. Halfway to Auckland, the Hen and Chickens Islands lined up east to west, and those islands were smack in their path. The Chickens were small, insignificant, but Hen Island, the largest and tallest, just eight miles from the coast, was a worry. Andy shared what Grady had told him: sailing through the passage between Hen and the Whangārei Heads, a long, high cliff on the coast, was often the fastest. The wind could accelerate between the two.

"All good," Sargent said, "but of course whatever we do, Koonce will do the opposite. He's got nothing to lose. There's no one close behind him, so we better be right." They went over it a dozen more times in the several hours before they had to pick a course to go inside or outside Hen Island. The wind lightened up a bit but remained relatively steady northeast.

There was little new information. The smart course kept reading inside. All three agreed. "If this costs me another goddamn case of rum, I am gonna be pissed," Sargent said as he cast his vote for inside.

"Aren't you one up on him?" Andy asked.

"Yeah, and being two up would be just fine."

It was one of those days. Hen Island decided to block the wind instead of accelerating it. *All American*'s speed dropped slowly from eight to five knots as Hen Island drew abeam. Sargent sat at the nav table, disbelieving. The mood on the boat was grim. "Complaining isn't going to fix it!" Sargent barked when he heard Caskie Kolegeri bitching. "So shut the hell UP!" That had put a lip-lock on the group. But it was hard not to grouse when *Ram* came out from behind Hen Island with its chute full and a decent head of steam up. In just a couple of wrenching hours, Koonce and company had held the stronger breeze outside, sailed an extra mile in the process, and caught up. Once free of Hen's block, *All American* picked up the breeze and matched Ram's speed.

Damaris was at his nav table looking ahead again. The rest of the crew were on deck, taking turns constantly trimming the big chute and the main, tweaking the vang, and moving weight around to squeeze every fraction of a knot out of the boat.

"We're going to have a beat into Auckland," Damaris told Sargent. "Our reaction to the late-afternoon shift will be key."

"Number one?" Sargent asked.

"Yes."

Four crewmen moved the big number one jib in its turtle from below to the deck ever so slowly so as not to disturb the boat's attitude in the water. As the sail was moved forward into position on the weather side, crewmen moved aft and to leeward to maintain the angle of heel that seemed fast. Joe Dugan, the lightest crewman, went forward briefly to attach the halyard and start the head of the sail into the pre-feeder. He then attached the sheets. With the binoculars, Sargent watched similar go-ings-on aboard *Ram Bunctious*. He cracked a smile. This should be good.

"Listen up," Sargent said. "Pete expects a shift down the road a piece, and a headwind into the finish. Tacking duel. Number one is ready. Crouse and Eric on the hoist, Zimmer trim with Larry. Dugan on the takedown, Caskie and Hoop gathering. Get it right. Smooth. Keep speed up. Now we wait."

Separated by about a mile, the two boats raced neck and neck under spinnaker for more than two hours. There was nothing in it for either of them as they exchanged boat-length leads. As one, they felt the shift. Both crews trimmed, and carefully sailed into the new wind, which was backing to come dead ahead. As one, jibs were hoist-ed and trimmed. Spinnakers came down. Crew work was flawless on both boats. Both had been on port tack. They both came off to the right of course, staying on port, a move that put *All American* inshore and to leeward of *Ram* with a sudden, if small, lead. At the wheel, Andy was comfortable being inside, thinking they might pick up a nice lift along the beach. *Ram* tacked away. For them to follow *All American* made no sense.

"Should we cover," Andy wondered.

Damaris: "Not enough advantage."

Sargent: "Hate not staying in the same water with them."

Andy: "The beach looks good. And here we are."

Sargent: "Stay with it, then. Make the best of it. Agree?"

Damaris and Andy agreed.

An hour later, they tacked. In another hour, *Ram* came into view, having tacked back. Stu was steering.

"We'll cross them, it looks," Stu said.

Sargent: "The right's paying off. Stay with it."

Stu tacked the boat when *Ram* was dead astern. They were close. Maybe three or four boat lengths.

It was thirty minutes before Andy would relieve Stu at the helm. He went below for one of his patented alpha naps. He was soon transported back six years, when he'd been on Mitch's boat off Newport, Rhode Island, trimming the jib and calling a close cross coming up with Koonce, who had the right of way. Andy was an overweight, out-of-shape wiseass at the time, thinking he'd make it hot for his hateful father by causing a near collision, saying they had room to cross, no problem, until it was an emergency helm down RIGHT NOW or watch his father's boat drive full speed into the cockpit of Koonce's boat and maybe kill somebody. "TACK NOW!!!" Andy had yelled, finally, and the great Mitchell Thomas, oh so cool Mitch who was admired by everyone, totally freaked out. Mitchell, screaming curses, had in fact put the helm down hard, and disaster had been avoided. But Mitchell Thomas had lost the race, which had been the whole idea. Then Andy had gotten drunk at the award dinner that had followed, opened his big mouth, and here he was. He opened his eyes. Here he was on this crazy round-the-world race boat, and out there was Koonce, once again, with both boats on the wind, playing opposite sides of the racecourse, with a winner-take-all cross coming up. Once again. Seahog Day. Only this time, it would be Andy at the wheel, because Mitch, his pretend father, was in jail for murdering his mother. And this time, he'd be on starboard tack with the right of way.

Ram Bunctious and *All American* were coming together again on opposite tacks. *Ram* from seaward, on port. American from the land side, on starboard.

"Looks like he's gotten a bit of a lift," Damaris said, studying *Ram* with binoculars. "Close. Gonna be close. He may be laying the finish line."

"If we can, I'd like to go at him, make him tack, then tack as he tacks," Andy said from the wheel. "That would finish him off."

"Never happen. He'll dip to take your stern."

"Got it."

The boats got closer, both moving at around eight knots in the moderate wind.

"Hard to tell," Damaris said, "but my guess is he's laying it."

Andy: "He can't cross us. We've got him."

Sargent: "He'll dip if he's laying it. If he's not he could dip anyway, then tack back at us on starboard."

"Be ready to do the best tack we've ever done," Andy said quietly. "Tell 'em, Joe."

From his position trimming the jib, Joe Dugan calmly called, "Starboard," just loud enough for *Ram* to hear it.

Damaris and Sargent were watching Koonce like hawks.

"Hunt him a little," Sargent said, meaning steer off and make him consider tacking.

Andy steered down four degrees. Koonce held course. Sargent: "He's definitely laying the finish."

Andy came back up. *Ram* suddenly turned down to dip.

"Now," Andy and Sargent said together. Andy tacked the boat at just the right speed, fast enough to get quickly onto the new tack, smooth enough to keep momentum, which was critical. *Ram* had a head of speed. *All American* would slow down in the tack. But light as it was, the boat would accelerate quickly. Andy held the boat off the wind a few degrees. The trimmers were with him, waiting to fine-tune until the speed came back up.

Koonce drove off, going fast, putting two boat lengths' distance between *Ram* and American. It was a great reaction to American's sudden tack, because when he came back on course to the finish, the two boats were dead even. And Ram's wind was clear.

For thirty minutes the two boats raced like they were stuck together. Spectator boats had been gathering for the past hour. Now there were hundreds of them as American and *Ram* approached Rangitoto Island and the finish. For the most part the spectators were behaving. Any bad wakes they created had an equal effect on the race boats.

"Want some good news?" Damaris asked. "The left side of the finish is favored. Shoot at just the right moment and we should nail him."

"Stu," Andy said, "how about taking the bow and giving me a signal. Wait until we are close." Stu gave Andy a thumbs-up and moved quietly to the mid-deck.

With fifty yards to go, Stu moved forward and lay facedown on the deck, his eyes even with the forward edge of the bow. The line was short, relatively easy to judge. He saw his counterpart on Ram, one hundred feet away, doing the same thing. *Ram* looked to have a slight edge. Getting close. Closer. Stu suddenly flung his hand out to the left, his pointing finger saying, Do it!

As one, both boats came head to wind, their momentum carrying them over the line. There was a gun and a whistle separated by less than two seconds. The crews of both boats exploded in cheers that were drowned out by the cacophony of horns, whistles, and yelling from the spectator boats.

"Who won it?!" The hail to the race committee came from Ram.

"*All American*," came the answer across the water.

Andy was wrung out, unbelieving. He looked across the water at Koonce and shrugged. Koonce looked back, then extended his arm in Andy's direction. His thumb came up.

IX

JODI

Isha had her eyes closed, the better to remember that afternoon on *Orion* when she'd first met with RD, the better to try and ignore the alarming, bumpy ride in the small twin-engine airplane from Barbados to the Caribbean island of Mustique. The flight on *Orion* owner Mark Creighton's private jet had been a treat, even for a person frightened of flying. Isha could certainly get used to that means of travel, with the three Cs: comfort, caviar, and champagne. But this horrible little plane was a relic, and it flew like one. It felt like an old bus on a bad road. Only over water. Mustique was supposed to be ultrachic, and this crummy little plane from Barbados was the only way to get there? Eyes closed and hope you survived.

Isha recalled that she and RD had in fact downed a few drinks sitting in the elegant surroundings that only a grand wooden yacht of the 1930s, maintained to the max, could provide. The gorgeous woodwork on all sides was superbly crafted and finished with a soft patina. The immaculate white overhead with its beaded longitudinals over oak frames, the teak and holly sole, the leaded stained glass on the cabinet doors, the matte varnished ash and mahogany, the polished brass hardware, and the soft leather cushions created an environment as old-world cozy as it was refined. And it smelled so good. Like money, Isha mused. She was entranced by how beautiful it was, how special it felt to be surrounded by such hand-crafted luxury. And on a boat! Who would have known. She couldn't imagine being underway, bouncing along on the ocean. No thank you. But tied to the dock in this well-protected cove, with just the faintest motion indicating that you were actually afloat, it was very pleasant indeed.

It hadn't taken RD long to come around. She'd had that pegged. He was gruff at first, but it was an act. Revenge was one of those animals that slept soundly but awoke quickly, ready to bite. She could only imagine what it was like to get shoved off a race boat into the water by the owner in front of the whole crew. Not cool, Andy, letting your own revenge dominate your good sense. It was one of those mistakes that would come back to haunt you. Another peril of revenge: it never ends.

She knew RD was going to play. What surprised her was how good a player he was, how quickly his ideas took shape and got hammered into workable moves. RD was clever. He understood there were too many variables to construct a complete game plan. It was enough that the two of them shared the same goal, which was to soundly disrupt whatever it was Andy and Becky had going. RD immediately understood Isha's plan to move ahead in some direction that could intercept Andy's path, to put themselves in a position to move quickly when the time was right. As RD had said, Florida was key: "Our good luck is, we know exactly where Andy is, where he is going, and when he's going to be there. He's just arrived at Auckland. Next will be around Cape Horn to Punta del Este, Uruguay. Then Florida in mid-April."

Hoping for a more immediate strike against Andy, Isha had trouble with that concept at first. But she soon realized RD was making sense. Take some time, work on acquiring a strong, flexible position, get some cash together because they would need it, and wait for an opening. Meanwhile, have some fun along the way. Fun! There was a new concept. But why not? And Florida made sense. RD knew the Miami/Fort Lauderdale boating scene like the back of his hand. As he had said, you can get anything done in Fort Lauderdale.

Isha and RD had met regularly. It wasn't long before he had made his move on her, but she held back. When she needed that card, she'd play it. But after her resistance he had stepped back. That was a surprise she wasn't sure she liked. But RD had really earned his keep when he suggested that Isha become a therapist/companion for the Creightons' granddaughter, Jodi. As Isha had heard at the hair salon, the spoiled teenager had been caught shoplifting, and that was the tip of her unstable iceberg. Her parents had died in their small plane when she was fourteen. Alcohol had reportedly been involved.

Jodi had gone to live with her grandparents. Now she was eighteen, a walking, seductive little package of anger, insecurity, and aggression that was way beyond the older Creightons' ability to cope with. RD said Jodi often hung around the boat, flirting with him, with no doubt about what she had in mind. Despite his weakness for women, RD had steered clear of getting involved. His job would be on the line, of course, but he also saw red flags all over the place.

It had taken Isha a while to get used to the therapist/companion idea. She'd discussed it with Cameron at one of their sessions. He'd laughed at first, then gotten serious. "You are not a therapist," he'd told her. "Pretending to be one isn't at all funny, not to mention it being very illegal. That's too much even for someone with your, pardon me, caustic attitude about life. You start trying to give what you think is therapy to some damaged, bonkers teenage girl and even you could be crushed by the mess that results."

"But you could help me," Isha suggested.

"Not for one second."

He'd been more willing to accept "companion."

"Given what you seem to have gone through, you might be able to help her as a companion," Cameron told Isha. "Mainly by listening. But beware. I know Mark Creighton. He's an old fossil-fuel fossil. There aren't many tougher guys. He eats people like you for lunch. Be very careful." Isha appreciated the advice. She didn't mention that what she had in mind for Jodi was more along the lines of co-option than help. An angry girl with her aggressive behavior pattern — and her money — could be useful.

Once Isha had agreed, RD went into action. Mark Creighton loved his boat, and was in the habit of going on board frequently. He'd gotten used to talking with his longtime captain about matters nautical that sometimes verged on the personal. It was a habit he'd mistakenly continued with RD, for whom everything was grist for his self-serving mill. For Creighton, the old adage applied: what is said on the boat stays on the boat. RD would have found that notion mildly amusing. One day the old man seemed unusually quiet, preoccupied. When RD cautiously inquired, Creighton had shaken his head and indicated that living with a renegade, troublesome teenager was giving him and his wife fits, that he was too bloody old to understand what was going on in her mind and wished he knew what to do about it. RD carefully ventured in at that point, saying friends of his had a similar problem they'd solved with a therapist/companion. He could find out more about it if Creighton wished. He did. RD primed a friend and gave his name to Isha to use as a reference.

Isha's interview with the old man had gone well. She had dressed conservatively, but nothing less than a space suit could have concealed her charms. She'd done some research on Creighton, which was easy enough. He and his wife had been regulars on the Manhattan/Greenwich, Connecticut, society circuit for many years. A prominent capitalist, and a friend and backer of President George H. W. Bush, Creighton had a fondness for women that was well known. There had been headlines and photographs here and denials there, all very politically spun, with Mrs. Creighton always standing smiling and supportive beside her husband.

Isha had been right. During the interview, which lasted far longer than it should have, Creighton's eyes had been busy. He had to be in his midseventies, with thinning gray hair and a well-lined, habitually tanned face. He kept himself fit, no doubt with a personal trainer. She had stressed the companionship aspect of how she could help Jodi. Creighton liked that approach. "I also look forward to getting to know you better," he had said, his eyes tinged with lust. "I could use a little companionship myself." When Isha had taken her leave, he had put a fatherly hand on her shoulder that had then made its way slightly below her waist. She had reacted subtly, in a not unfriendly way.

When the aged Beechcraft King Air banked and began its final descent, Isha knew why this small airplane was used for Mustique. She'd never seen such a short landing strip. It looked no bigger than a football field, and the first two hundred feet were on a downhill slant, oh my God. Eyes closed again. Beside her, Jodi looked up from the catalog she was browsing. "It's okay, really," Jodi said, and took her hand.

It had been a strange start with Nina for Jodi, whose grandmother, Nancy Creighton, had broken the news about her new "companion." Jodi had been furious, but knew better than to resist her clueless grandparents' latest attempt to normalize her. Normalize, whatever the hell that meant. She did the usual "Yes Gram," and figured this companion crap would run its short, ugly course like the rest of the ridiculous therapeutic fixes they had tried. Jodi had played along when she was told this Nina woman was coming to take her to lunch. Surprise. Nina certainly wasn't the middle-aged priss she'd expected. Au contraire. Jodi liked the Porsche, and the cool way Nina drove it, like she was being chased by the cops.

But Jodi was stumped by this woman's presence. She'd expected an uptight professional of some sort intent upon sounding her out, getting inside her head. She'd been working on some wild stuff to tell her. Instead, here was this sexy creature out of a film noir with an amazing body, a face that could stop traffic, and a puzzling, almost rude way of ignoring her. Other than hello, and her name, Nina hadn't said anything. She just drove until she'd skidded the Porsche to a stop at a funky ribs joint off the highway. Another surprise. Jodi knew her grandmother had made a reservation for them at her club.

Nina had turned off the car, pulled the keys from the ignition, and unfastened her seat belt. Then she'd turned to Jodi and said, "So what'd you grab?"

Jodi: "Excuse me?"

"What'd you grab when you got busted?"

Jodi regarded this woman, not believing her ears. Nina was not looking friendly. What the hell! Jodi paused, then said quietly, "Panties. A three-pack."

Nina held her icy stare on Jodi. Then she burst out laughing. "Panties?" she said after her amusement had finally subsided. "Panties?! You're gonna rip someone off and get busted in the process for a nineteen-ninety-five three-pack of panties? That's the best you can do? Really? You've got a lot to learn, girl. Come on. Let's get some ribs." By the end of a two-hour lunch and a couple of bottles of beer, Jodi had been hooked by this nutty woman who had spent most of the time talking about herself. Jodi had hardly gotten a word in edgewise.

Three or four times a week Nina would arrive at the Creightons' to pick up Jodi. They'd watched some movies, cruised the malls and shopped, smoked a bunch of weed, and mostly talked. One afternoon Jodi had asked Nina just what she was supposed to be. "I mean, my grandparents hired you, right?"

"Right."

"What's your job? Are you like a shrink? Do you report back about me?"

"I am paid to be your companion. How you behave is report enough. You continue to be a jerk, I'll probably get terminated. You settle down, stop acting like a spoiled rich brat, and everyone's happy."

"I never knew there was such a job. Pretty easy money."

"Not always. What if you were a creep? And there's your grandfather. He'd like to get in on it."

"No kidding. You're hot. I'm sure he'd like that. Why not? Another notch in his gun. Doubt he gets much at home."

The King Air came to a stop near the small bamboo building that served as the Mustique terminal, and shut down. Isha opened her eyes. Miraculously, everyone was alive. The head of the Mustique Company was on hand to greet Creighton, one of the island's most important landowners and a board member to boot. The staff of his Goliath House was on hand with several Kawasaki Mules to transfer luggage and people. Jodi had been going to

Mustique for years, and waved at several local boys along the dirt roads that went by house after glorious house. All of them could have been from the pages of Architectural Digest. "Rosco always has the best herb," Jodi said quietly to Nina after she'd greeted one very attractive man.

An hour later, Isha and Jodi had unpacked their belongings in the guesthouse on the property and were stretched out by the pool in their bikinis, sipping Banana Touches that had been served by Tomas the butler, a friendly young man Jodi knew. He quietly told her to check her bedside table. She thanked him profusely, explaining to Isha after he left that all the staff were from Saint Vincent, the big island capital of Saint Vincent and the Grenadines, of which Mustique was a part. "They let Mustique do its thing as long as they pay plenty of taxes and hire Saint Vincentians," she said. "All the herb is grown in the mountains in Saint Vincent, and it's the best."

Isha was taking in the handsome expanse of Goliath House, a large, six-bedroom, U-shaped dwelling that wrapped around three sides of the pool. Thick green foliage and flowers were everywhere, growing rapidly twelve months a year. There was no glass in most of the windows, cleverly designed to avoid rain. Mosquitoes, the island's namesake — once in profusion — were now under chemical control. Birds were everywhere. Regal frigate birds drifted majestically against the fluffy clouds, a thousand feet overhead. The wide-eyed Bequia sweets were coming in close, calling and stretching their beaks skyward, boldly stealing peanuts from the little bowl Tomas had left.

The house was on one of the many hilltops on the island. The view of azure-blue ocean to the horizon that extended the clean drop-off of the infinity pool was hypnotic. Jodi was on a roll, talking about the island, how the seventy homes represented owners from thirty different countries, and saying that after dinner they would hop on a scooter and go hang with Rosco and his friends, when Isha caught the subtle flash of a reflection coming from the direction of the house. She stole a glance and saw the unmistakable shadow of Mark Creighton with binoculars raised in their direction. As she adjusted her position to give Creighton a more enticing view, Isha told Jodi her plan sounded like fun. Fun, she thought, feeling the rum taking hold, feeling the sun warming her body, feeling Creighton's eyes on her. Fun. That word again. Let's have it.

X

SAM

"Look, Andy, it's great you won the leg. I can't wait to hear every bloody detail, I don't care it if takes three Scotches. Everyone here is delighted. Great publicity. The response is very good, better than anyone expected, to be honest. And Becky's pictures, wonderful. There's just one problem. You're the CEO of Moss Optics, at least for the moment. The guy in charge. You have to show your face around here every so often. No way around it."

It was Sam on the phone. Andy was listening, getting a little lecture about responsibility, and not enjoying it. It would be so easy to blow Sam off, stay in Auckland, where Andy had become an overnight celebrity for beating Koonce at his own game; Auckland, where his money was no good in any bar or restaurant once he'd been recognized. New Zealand was such a cool place. It was so remote. In many ways it really was another world. The land was impressive, so marvelously varied that it was impossible to ignore. From the striking fjords, the fertile Canterbury Plains, and the snow-covered mountains of the South Island to the amazing rock formations on the beaches of the North, Mother Nature had done some of her best work here. It was all gorgeous, a sportsman's paradise with 400 golf courses, a friendly place to live. Life here seemed just a touch more relaxed than anywhere else Andy had ever been. More sheep than people, they said, and according to a local joke, men were men and the sheep were worried. Probably more boats than people, at least as many. Andy and Becky had snuck off one afternoon and looked at houses. But he was listening. He knew Sam was right.

"There are some big decisions coming up, and a few overly ambitious people with friends on the board who I know have their eyes on your job. Unless you don't care. But I think you do."

Andy assured Sam he cared.

"Then you need to get on the next plane, damn it, get your butt back here and pretend you know what's going on. I'll send you a file; you can catch up on the plane. You'll have plenty of time." Sam laughed.

"Only around twenty hours," Andy said. "Okay, okay, you're right, Sam. I'll let you know the schedule."

Gloria, Andy's secretary, and his pal Jeff Linn met him and Becky at JFK. That was such an odd pairing that Andy immediately sensed a problem. Jeff had been as intimidated by Gloria as Andy had, maybe more so. They didn't come more officious than Gloria, or more capable, or more enticing in a militaristic sort of way. She presented a very unfair combination. Andy had always thought Gloria could run the company. She was doing a pretty good job in his absence. But things had changed at Moss, and for the better. With Mitchell gone and Sam more or less in charge, Jeff had told him, a new atmosphere prevailed at the company. The grim, oppressive tone set by Mitch had been replaced by a more productive, community-wide energy. Smiling had almost become a trend. But these two employees didn't look happy. Their greeting was perfunctory. Jeff was studying his shoes. Gloria was on point, as usual.

"Sam . . . your dad," Gloria said to Becky, "is in the hospital. I'm so sorry. It happened while you were in the air."

Becky was aghast. Her father was in his eighties with a heart condition, playing well into the fourth quarter. Even so, it's impossible to comprehend or accept impending loss. The inevitable is always in denial. A sudden turn for the worse is always a painful surprise. "What happened?"

"Heart," Gloria said. "On the golf course."

Becky put her face in her hands. "We should go to the hospital directly."

"Soon as you pick up your bags."

"You should have seen that baby," Sam said from his bed. He looked tired, but his voice had that old crackle. "One of my best drives ever, well over two hundred yards, straight as an arrow. What a sound. Craack! I'll never forget that one." He paused. "I ended up on the ground." He chuckled, then looked disappointed. "Could have been par."

"Dad, try to rest."

"Plenty of time for that. Plenty of time."

Andy was dozing in the comfort of a first-class accommodation. He had taken a Halcion, and it had kicked in nicely. Sam had died the following day, closed his eyes and expired peacefully after having had a last talk with Andy and Becky that was mostly about golf, including some light-headed musings about what the golf courses in his future might be like. Would the rough be a tangle, or friendly? Would the greens be fast? Would drives carry five or six hundred yards on those rarefied links? Would the traps be fluffy and dry, immaculately raked like Japanese sand gardens? It had been tough on Becky, but what a good way to go, Andy thought, hoping he'd be half as amused when it was his turn.

At Sam's behest, there was no funeral. The outpouring of condolences had been impressive. From Harvard alumni and military mates to business friends and golf partners, the immense response was testament to the wide and gracious swath Sam had cut through a productive and considerate life. His law degree had gotten him a commission in the Navy in the early 1940s. He'd served aboard a destroyer and survived several harrowing forays, none of which appeared to have created permanent damage, physically or psychologically. He was living proof, Andy thought, that a substantial business could be run with congeniality, that even lawsuits could be settled without an excess of ham-fisted vitriol. But for the most part, that was then. Andy wondered if Sam might have been among the last of his breed. Or maybe he was just unique, one of a kind.

Andy had had his moment with the board, calling an emergency session so he could catch a plane in time to make the next leg of The Race. That hadn't been as bad as expected, probably thanks to Sam's death. Grief temporarily tabled whatever contestable items might have been lurking on personal agendas. Andy had reported on The Race. He was praised, was told Race promotion had been very good for the company's retail products, their binoculars and small scopes. He had been encouraged to continue as long as he agreed to make an appearance between legs. It had all been quite uneventful, save for his amazement that Mountain View, his old concept for an astronomy-themed hotel complex, was being considered by the board. Mitch had crushed the idea, and Andy had figured it would stay crushed. But there it was, and he had to admit it was still exciting, the idea of a Martian-styled hotel campus built around a high-end telescope of the sort Jeff had designed for Andy's house.

Everything about the Mountain View concept reeked of outer space — of the universe — from drinks like a Black Hole (dark rum and iced coffee with a dash of sweet vermouth) to air-lock sound effects when doors opened and closed to every guest's choice of what expanse of the night sky they would sleep under. Guests would be allotted time on the telescope, supervised by astronomy grad students. Andy queried one of the board members after the meeting, who told him that Mountain View had not been fully evaluated, but that thanks to Gloria they had his old plans, and several members thought it would be a smart promotion for Moss, a natural follow-up to the company's new public presence thanks to The Race. Gloria at work.

He was flying alone. Becky had her hands full as executor of her father's estate. Neither of them liked it. They hadn't been apart for several months. She planned to meet him in Punta del Este, Uruguay, their next stop. He hoped Punta would be friendlier than the first time they had stopped there. That was a bad movie, being sent to that very rough neighborhood bar by Isha, his desperate fight with the guy with a knife, all set up by Mitch and executed by his nasty girlfriend, Andy's ex-girlfriend . . . Whoa, he had to change channels. The intense white noise of the Boeing 747's engines and of the hull tearing through thin air at nearly six hundred miles an hour dragged Andy into another disturbing scene, this one with his skipper, Jan Sargent, who had discovered the tube of jewels buried in the missing keel bolt. Sargent was ballistic.

"You think I wouldn't know about something, anything, on my fucking boat?" Sargent's veins were bulging. He was at full tilt. Andy felt Sargent's spittle raining on his face. "That there would be a spare roll of goddamn electrical tape or toilet paper on my boat that would escape my fucking attention? We are now smuggling jewels in addition to racing around the world? You son-of-a-bitch stupid rich kid . . . what in Christ were you thinking? And removing a keel bolt . . . Jesus! . . . you don't think there's a reason they put in ten bolts? Five pair? So now maybe the keel has a better chance of ripping off if we should happen to hit one of those growlers that fall off icebergs, and we roll over and fucking die. All of us. You asshole! You don't have enough money? Is that the problem?"

"My father . . ." Andy muttered.

"Your father?! Grady? Your father tells you to kill someone, you're gonna do it?"

"How . . ."

"You don't think we check the keel bolts after every leg? They can get loose, you didn't know that, especially on a light, unseaworthy piece of shit like we are racing on. This boat is a big freaking dinghy, not made for blue-water racing by anyone's stretch of the imagination. And you removed a keel bolt!"

Sargent suddenly drew back his fist and launched it at Andy's face. Andy ducked, flung up his arms to ward off the blow.

"Sir, please, sir . . ."

Andy awoke to the flight attendant trying to calm him down. He could barely get his eyes open. The Halcion was far from done with him. But he could focus enough to realize he'd made quite a mess of his area. The flight attendant was gathering up papers, books, and magazines that had gone flying into the aisle.

"Whoa, sorry, sorry," Andy mumbled.

"No problem, sir. Must have had a bad dream."

"For sure," Andy said, closing his eyes, returning to Halcion's fervid embrace. The flight attendant pulled up his blanket.

Dreams that mimic reality will linger, haunt you. One of the first things Andy did upon arriving in Auckland was visit the boat. It was midnight when he landed. He drove to the yard, showed his pass to the gatekeeper, whom he had to wake up, and was soon pulling up the cabin sole. It was crazy, he knew, and everything was un-disturbed, of course, the way he and Martin had left it, but he simply had to make sure.

Andy was half-conscious for the crew meeting the next morning. The sixteen-hour time change was brutal. The boys were glad to see him. They expressed sadness about Sam. Sargent ran the meeting.

"Two days to the start," Sargent said. "We're good. We could start this afternoon. That's what happens when you guys bust your asses. Everything's ready except for perishables — eggs, milk, fruit, and some bacon for Bo-sworth — that will be delivered late tomorrow."

Teddy Bosworth, the closest thing they had to a cook, had a big smile. "I'll share," he said, "really."

"The issue," Sargent continued, "as always, will be the weather. Harder to predict as we sail south. We've got Cape Horn this leg. There's a gale there every four days, on average, and, well, let's hope we play the odds right. Damaris has got some ideas. No doubt our esteemed owner will have a few. Andy?"

"Thanks for the good thoughts about Sam," Andy said. "You'll be glad to know he went down swinging — a golf club." The group chuckled. "He wouldn't have wanted it any other way. He went out imagining the golf courses in his next life, when work wouldn't get in the way. I'll tell you, the guys at Moss, meaning the board of directors, are very happy about how we are doing. The press has been very good, and lucky you, the Moss guys gave me permission to come back."

Andy was eager to be off to the gym to give his muscles a chance to regroup after ten days of inactivity and the long flight, but he stayed to have another coffee with Sargent and catch up. The skipper said the crew was in good shape. Larry Kolegeri had gotten in a bit of trouble when he chatted up the wrong girl at a bar one night. Turned out to be somebody's wife. Somebody important. It caused a near donnybrook, but cool heads and apologies had prevailed.

"And we came this close to moving the keel," Sargent said. "Stu was for it, and so was driver Crouse, and Zimmer the trimmer. Both of them thought the balance could be improved a touch if we moved it forward. Just a smidge. We had ten days, could have done it, barely, but we could have. We got the designer, Gibb Frey, on the phone. He did some numbers and agreed it might help, but he was talking two, maybe three inches max. And for what it was gonna cost, it surely would have given Sam a heart attack well before he hit that drive. For three inches I scrubbed it. If it's not broken . . ."

Andy was hoping the color hadn't drained from his face, and that if it had, Sargent hadn't noticed, or thought it was caused by the time change. He hoped he'd remained composed, that his jaw hadn't sagged open, that he hadn't drooled. He realized he had to say something.

"And if you'd decided to do it, you would have called me, of course."

"Of course," Sargent said with an evasive smile. A good workout helped Andy clear his head and focus on the leg ahead. But on the short afternoon sail to go over the sail inventory, he found himself distracted at the wheel. He had put Moss Optics out of his mind, and now there it was, with Mountain View to think about again. And there was that little can buried in the keel. He'd more or less forgotten about that as well until the frightening Halcion-stoked dream had floored him. And they had actually considered moving the keel! Of all the far-out, unexpected possibilities he'd totally failed to consider. He supposed he could have stopped it, but what if Sargent had just dealt with Sam and gone ahead with it? It made him sick to think about it. And there was Becky, who he'd come to rely on, a world away. He'd call her when they got in.

"Ground control to Captain Andy." It was Damaris. "Hello, anyone home? We were just saying, several times actually, it might be a good idea to head for the barn, have a drink, get some chow."

"Sorry, guys. It's still yesterday for me. Tacking . . ."

Andy skipped the details, but he did tell Becky about the dream, and about how Jan had stunned him with the possibility of moving the keel.

"I have to admit, I've had some very bad minutes," he said to her.

There was a pause, never a good sign with Becky. "I have to accept what you've done, well, because I do," Becky said. "But listen, Andy, you can't come whining to me for sympathy, because honestly, I don't have any. You know how I feel about it. That's not going to change. My advice is to forget about it because it's already done and there's no undoing it. You know the old line — if you can't do the time, don't do the crime. Says it all. So stop feeling sorry for yourself. Forget it. Like you said, someone snuck on the boat and did this. That's not bad. Go with it. Don't waste any more time on it. It's done. Over. Get it together. Race the boat. Throw those stupid dreams overboard."

"I wasn't whining."

"Oh, Andy . . ."

"You're right."

"I know."

"I love you."

"Not as much as I love you."

XI

COCKTAILS

"You drive," Jodi said. "I love the way you drive."

The Mule was no Porsche, but its wide stance and strong low gears made it just right for Mustique's rough dirt roads. Isha followed the other Mule, driven by Tomas, with the Creightons as passengers, and listened to Jodi rant about the cocktail parties on Mustique.

"It's all pretty boring here in general," Jodi said, "unless you love going to the beach. There's a few horses and a couple tennis courts. Period. But the cocktail parties are maybe the worst. When the owners are here in season, which is now, the same forty people show up at a different house every week and talk about their houses, how they just got their humongous, ten-foot-wide ceramic planters delivered from Italy, or how their new hundred-thousand-dollar La Cornue stove just arrived from France. It's all such petty bullshit. Not like last night. That was fun."

Isha had to agree. They'd gone to visit Jodi's friend Rosco in the village, where fifty or so indigenous residents of Mustique resided. The village consisted of a store, a bar, and a few modest houses arranged around a church. She'd learned that keeping the village intact was another part of the Mustique Company's deal with Saint Vincent. Many of the residents were descendants of the handful of people who had been scratching out a living for many years, growing cotton and fishing, before a remittance man, Colin Tennant — a British peer also known as Lord Glenconner — had purchased Mustique in the 1960s. He'd given a piece of land on the island to his friend, HRH Princess Margaret, and that brilliant move had helped the island become an exclusive getaway. It was camping out at first, with generators that frequently failed and swarms of bloodthirsty mosquitoes, but it was slumming at its most exotic — with the rebel princess!

Isha had been amazed at how welcoming Rosco and his friends had been. She and Jodi had spent a pleasant evening smoking weed, drinking cold beer, and listening to stories of the island's early days. Glenconner, quite a flake by all accounts, had loved themed costume parties. The naughtier the better. Jodi said Colin aspired to emulate earlier British sybarites like those decadent socialites who took their wild fun and games to Kenya's Happy Valley in the 1930s. "My grandmother has told me all about them," Jodi said. "She said they practiced 'weapons-grade hedonism.' Not sure what it means, but love that expression. Wish I could have been there."

Rosco's friend Charlie told a story about how his

father and several friends had been tasked by Glenconner to take inflatable dolls into the surf and appear to have sex with them during one racy gathering. Alas, the dolls had deflated.

Isha couldn't recall a more relaxed evening. A week or two on Mustique and she'd forget why she was there.

"The homeowners these days couldn't care less," Jodi said. "They just want to complain, complain about the help, complain about the food that has to be brought over from Saint Vincent on the ferry, complain about some stupid fancy refrigerator they're waiting for. I wouldn't be going to one of these parties unless you were here. Well, maybe I would, this one anyway, to see Jocko. But you'll meet some high rollers. You don't have a place here unless you are up to your neck in green. These are world-class high rollers, big money dumpers, like the guy who invented the barcode, for instance, the guy who invented the scuba regulator for diving, people like that. People like my grandfather, who is single-handedly poisoning the world with fossil fuels and making kazillions doing it. I'll introduce you to Jocko. He's into diamonds. It's his party. I'm one of his favorites, if you know what I mean." She turned her head and flipped an earring that sparkled.

"Really?" Isha gave Jodi the eye.

"Really." She giggled.

"Sounds risky."

"Oh, it is," she gushed. "I love it."

Jocko's piece of Mustique consisted of a main dwelling surrounded by several outbuildings, and the pool, of course. If there was one thing the houses of Mustique seemed to have in common, Isha observed, it was concrete. It was necessary, Jodi had told her, given the heavy salt-air beating everything took every day. Salt air and tropical sun is a brutal pairing. The trick was the creative use of the concrete. On one house the finish looked like marble. On another it was shaped into decorative exterior corner blocks (quoins), or made to look intricately carved with a variety of incorporated seashells.

Jocko's staff were parking the Mules when photographer Patrick Lichfield arrived on his motorcycle. Lichfield, also known as Patrick Anson, fifth Earl of Lichfield, first cousin once removed from Queen Elizabeth, returned Isha's stare with a winning smile. "Watch out for him," Jodi muttered. "He'll have your clothes off before you can sneeze."

People were roaming everywhere in the balmy evening, half hidden by the heavy tropical foliage and serenaded by the pulsing music of frogs and beetles. Jodi led the way to the main house, hoping to find Jocko. She introduced Isha to a few people along the way, then disappeared. Isha roamed, found herself staring at the simplistic finish of the interior of Jocko's house, disguised by the gorgeous furnishings that had to have been shipped in from Europe; at the bamboo floors; at the horizontal row of windows atop the living room walls; and at the ceiling, an intricate work of art.

"It's called a tray ceiling." The voice was velvety, with the trace of an accent, probably Italian.

"Nina, this is my friend Jocko." Jodi was clutching the arm of an engaging, athletic-looking gentleman in his forties who could have doubled for Johnny Depp in one of his more sinister roles. His facial hair was neatly trimmed. The large diamond around his neck on a gold chain was impossible to ignore. His black linen shirt was unbuttoned just right to show it off.

"Very pleased," he said, taking Isha's hand, holding her eyes with his. But it was a brief, cocktail-party greeting because a fellow named Sonny appeared. Sonny was quite high and on a roll. Sonny responded to Jodi's introduction of Isha with a quick nod in her direction; it was clear he was on a mission to talk with Jocko, whom he guided to one side so he could have that conversation.

"Sonny," Jodi said aside to Isha, "is a character, a tough little guy from Brooklyn who married well, thinks he has his finger on the pulse of the island, and maybe he does, because he's involved in everything. He got himself on the board. My grandfather hates him, duh. Rosco says Sonny is always asking him how much money he thinks he has in his pocket, that he'll give it to him if he comes within ten dollars."

"Does Rosco ever get it?"

"No. He won't play such a dumb game. He knows Sonny would lie if he happened to get it right. Plus it is so uncool it's almost cool, if you know what I mean."

"Creepy."

"But you can't dis Sonny. He knows too much. And he's friendly, funny, with those big blue eyes. He did time in LA, in the music business. Big user. Come on. We can snoop. They're just on the other side of that cane plant."

"Well yeah," Sonny was saying with that classic Brooklyn slur those guys must practice, "it should be big, but not ostentatious, ya know? I mean I don't want guys grabbin' it off her chest, ha ha. Whaddaya think, four carats, maybe five? Oval. How big is yours? Maybe not that big. Think oval would be right?"

Jodi rolled her eyes at Isha. "Let's go check out the pool, have a little smoke."

"Just a sec," Isha said, as Jocko finished talking and Sonny started to speak.

"I've been wanting to ask you," Sonny said, "somebody in your business, isn't smuggling a problem? Whaddaya do about that?"

"There's enough to go around."

"Yeah?"

"It's business, both sides. It's amusing."

"You play both sides?"

"Why not? Trying to stop it is impossible. Gets ugly. Why not take a piece of the action? Much less expensive, more fun. And tax free!"

"Damn. No kidding."

"Australia. There's a nice little scene going on down there. Guy I know is involved. He owns the mine. It's small, been going on twenty years. Well run. We'd all like a scene like that. There's a package right now on a race boat. Totally cool. Makes me smile."

"On a race boat. You gotta be kidding. I love it. On a race boat."

A few days later Isha found herself at Basil's Bar on what served as Mustique's harbor. It is a poor, unprotected excuse for a harbor. Ask anyone who has spent even one night anchored there in the sizable rollers that never seem to stop. Basil's itself is anchored on the rocks and built out over the water on pilings that seemed puny. It is thatch-roofed and appeared to be hastily hammered together, looking like any decent storm could wash it away. But year after year it's hung on. Isha and Jodi were at Basil's because word had come to the house that Creighton's boat, *Orion*, had arrived. And there was RD, sitting at a table with the three crew he'd hired for the delivery to Mustique, eating french fries and drinking a beer. Jodi had told Isha that fries with fresh lime wedges were the standard snack at Basil's. Avoid drinks with ice, she had cautioned. Heaven knew where that water came from.

Isha had to be careful. As far as the Creightons knew, she didn't know RD. Jodi took care of that, waltzing over with a big friendly greeting and a smooch for RD, and introducing Isha. Soon there were more fries, more beer, and lively conversation. When Mark and Nancy Creighton arrived, RD, Jodi, and Isha joined them at a separate table. Isha found herself sitting next to Mark, whose hand immediately found her leg.

Mark had made his move a few days before, offering Isha a very lucrative bonus for a weekly encounter. It was strictly business, monkey business couched as massage therapy, scheduled weekly at 3:00 p.m., when Mrs. Creighton's AA group met on the beach. Not that she would have cared, but protocol had to be observed. Isha considered it easy money and an insurance policy of sorts. She ignored Mark's hand. Mainly she was eager to have a talk with RD, who she hoped might find Jocko's comment about a package on a race boat interesting. She looked at *Orion* rocking in the harbor, its mast tips occasionally rolling through fifteen, twenty feet, and dreaded going on board. But how else could she talk with RD in private?

"Come for dinner at the house tonight," Creighton said to RD. "We can plan our little jaunt down islands."

"Yes sir. Thank you. I have a plan mapped out for you to look at."

"Very good."

Sitting below on *Orion*, Isha had to brace her feet to stay in place. Mark Creighton had actually suggested that RD show her the boat, and while she was eager to accept that kind invitation, her stomach was against it. Get it done and get the hell back on shore. But RD hadn't missed a beat. He was taking his time, enjoying having Isha at a disadvantage. He waxed on about the trip down, saying it had been quite uneventful. They had done it in ten days, not bad for the old girl. And was she sure he couldn't get her something to eat, or maybe a cooling rum swizzle?

Fighting to keep nausea at bay, Isha interrupted RD.

"I am not long for this world out here, as you well know, bastard, so just shut up and listen while I can still talk. There's a guy here, Jocko, a high roller. Diamonds. I overheard him talking about smuggling, saying guys like him get involved in that game, they buy in, it's just another way to make money, cheaper than trying to stop it. And more fun. Oh no . . ."

Isha stood up, made her way to the galley, hanging on, opened the trash container, and threw up.

"That will make you feel better," RD said. "There are

some crackers, saltines, right there in a jar on the counter. Eat a couple."

Isha grabbed a few crackers, sat back down, bit off a small piece, and tried to ignore RD's patronizing smile.

"Jocko said there's a cool smuggling scene in Australia, and that there's a package right now on a race boat. Does that mean anything to you, get your brain going at all?"

"No." RD paused. "But yeah, maybe. Australia, race boat — interesting combination, since the six boats in The Race are just about to leave there. What day is it? Tomorrow I think is the restart."

"And on one of those race boats is our friend Andy. Now get me the hell off this thing."

XII

CAPE HORN

Crouse was steering when *All American* struck something. It wasn't a hard hit. Having been drifting through a windless hole for more than six hours, a very rare condition considering their position, the boat had barely been making headway. The crew was a week into the leg they were sailing in the South Pacific Ocean. They were halfway between Auckland, New Zealand, and Cape Horn, a distance of 4,500 miles, about as far from land in any direction as possible on planet Earth, and afloat on the surface of roughly 5,000 feet of water. Talk about isolation. Colliding with anything in that location was cause for alarm. It wasn't a whale, always a threat. Hitting a whale would have produced a much bigger shock. More of a dull thud. Whatever they'd hit had a definite metallic resonance.

Andy awoke from a sound sleep with a start. The keel! He leaped up and grabbed a flashlight. It was around 2:00 a.m. and very dark. The slight contact had been enough to rouse the entire crew. To everyone's horror and amazement, they found themselves peering over the side at a container. Like a growler (a hunk of an iceberg about the size of a pickup truck), only one corner of the container was showing above water. The rest of the forty-foot-long steel box that weighed nearly three tons empty was partially visible beneath the surface. It was an ugly sight, lurking like a monster, menacing in its unlikely lair; a random disaster waiting to happen to some unsuspecting craft. Mostly full of water in addition to whatever was being shipped in it — there was no guessing what it actually weighed. *All American*'s keel had gently encountered the dread object, and the boat had nearly come to a stop as it slowly nudged its way along the container's side. Andy took a breath. The only damage to the keel would be a few scratches.

"I'll never complain again about not having any wind," Larry Kolegeri said quietly, staring dumbfounded at the thing that was wallowing obscenely in the calm waters.

"Imagine hitting that at twenty knots," Damaris said.

Eric was shooting video. "Or ten. Even five! Our good luck," he said, "all the numbers are on the side we can see. We'll soon know who this thing belongs to. They lose nearly a thousand of these things overboard every year, can you imagine?"

"Our good luck," Jan Sargent said, shaking his head. "I'll say. Put out a bulletin with a waypoint and the time," Sargent said to Eric. "Let everybody know it's in the area."

✳

The restart in Auckland had been uneventful other than the visit from a fast, forty-foot cruiser that had chased *All American* down an hour later. The boat had come in very close astern, much to Sargent's concern, until he saw the bikini-clad woman pressed against the cruiser's bow pulpit waving a present and shouting for Teddy Bosworth. Amid heavy commentary from his mates, Teddy went to the stern and accepted the gift without mishap. The cruiser quickly backed away with cries of "Come back, Teddy . . . I'll miss you" drifting across the water, cries the crew would take up unmercifully for the rest of the race.

The crew was heading for a bout with the Southern Ocean, the pièce de résistance of The Race. It would be the boys' second engagement with the planet's most challenging place to sail, let alone race: a thousand-mile-wide swath of two-mile-deep ocean encircling the globe between sixty degrees south and Antarctica. The fact that weather there is unimpeded by any continental land mass, not even a decent-sized island, makes these waters whimsically, and dangerously, active. Gale-force winds, storms, very large waves, even blizzards romp centrifugally around the Southern Ocean. The crew had sustained a good Southern Ocean whomping in a previous leg that had finished in Fremantle. That spinnaker knockdown, with the boat lying on its side for nearly a minute before the sail had been cut free, was one of those frightening sailing moments they would never forget. They had girded themselves for another invasion of this no-man's-sea.

Ask any of them about their primary motivation for coming on The Race and the answer would likely have

been the same: sailing the Southern Ocean. Just as moun-
taineers have their wish lists of ultimate places to climb
— Annapurna, K2 — ocean racers check off major events
like Sydney Hobart, Fastnet, and Transpac. But racing in
the Southern Ocean stands atop the list. If you are just
slightly out of your mind, you can tackle the Southern
Ocean double-handed on the Barcelona World Race,
which is nonstop. If one is truly beyond hope, he or she
can enter the single-handed Vendée Globe round-the-
world race, also nonstop, most of which is spent in the
Southern Ocean. A much more reasonable way to experience the Southern Ocean is to be part of a full, seasoned
crew on The Race, with stops every one to six thousand
miles to have hot showers, experience a new port, so-
cialize, and eat some fried chicken. And it's more fun to
celebrate the screaming reaches and share the inevitable
breakdowns, the often brutal weather, and various other
crises that probably will occur with a trusted and capable
team of similarly overly cranked sailors. For years afterward one can celebrate — reconfirm! — the adventure
over a pint with another gonzo bloke who was there. But
even with strong mates on either side, a barroom brawl is
still a barroom brawl. Heading into the Southern Ocean
will always increase one's heart rate.

All American's brush with the container was the
subject of conversation for several days. It was such a
frightening near miss. What could have been — the boat
holed and sinking quickly beneath their feet, serious in-
juries, the mast coming down, and many days in a life raft
if the thing even inflated — chilled their dreams. Once
they have put their lives in Mother Nature's hands, ocean

sailors are superstitious creatures. Collectively the crew kept wondering why they had been spared. It came up on Andy's watch one night. *All American* had finally escaped the little local doldrum and was heading south at a reasonable pace. It was quiet on deck, cold but relatively comfortable. Stu Samuels had put it best. "Mother Nature simply isn't that friendly," he said, "or that empathetic with us humans who are savaging her planet with carbon dioxide and floating containers. What in hell got into her to slow us down so we didn't get ripped apart by that thing?"

"Drugs," Damaris said. "She must have been smokin' weed again."

"Naw," Caskie said. "It's Jan. She loves Jan."

"I think it was Sam," Andy said. "Sam must have paid her a visit. He had a way with women."

"Seriously, you have to ask why," Stu persisted. "You do. We're not a bunch of choirboys. We're freaking sailors. We live selfish lives driven by the desire to be at sea. We're like those Joseph Conrad sailors who get in trouble when they're ashore for more than a couple days. Unless we're jibing the chute or trimming the backstay we're basically irresponsible wayfarers who drink too much and shirk normal responsibilities. Why'd she save our sorry asses?"

Nobody spoke for a while.

"I stole a car once," Kolegeri said. "I was drunk. Needed a ride. Hit a pole. Walked away."

"I purposely made a bad call," Andy said. "Port starboard situation, out to get my pretend father, said we could make it when I knew we couldn't. At the last second I told him to tack."

"And he did," Stu said.

"Yeah, but he might not have. Would have wrecked boats, killed people. Unforgivable. Stupid."

"And that is why we're here," Stu said.

For a while they listened to the water burbling past the hull, looked at the stars, and silently contemplated their own missteps.

"I got married," Damaris said. "Knew it was a bad idea. Did it anyway. Disaster."

The thought of Damaris being married made Stu laugh. "'Least you didn't have any kids."

"There was one time both my wife and my girlfriend were pregnant," Damaris said.

"Don't let Mother know that!" Stu said.

"Come on, guys," Sargent said. "Everybody's got skeletons. It's all random. The good, the bad, and the ugly all get cooked in the same pot. I just hope we haven't used up our luck."

They hadn't. Mother Nature blew away the calm with a more expected, freshening westerly that would peak at around twenty-five knots with higher gusts, driving *All American* toward Cape Horn with a vengeance. They had come out of Auckland and headed southeast, the smart strategy for picking up westerly storm tracks, or low-pressure systems that would push them in the right direction. They had run into the calm spot along the way.

Once hooked into the Low, the sailing was both exhilarating and exhausting. Damaris seemed to have put them in just the right place where they had encountered a strong Low and were able to stay in it. They were on the south side of the Southern Ocean, but not dangerously so. Go too far south and there would be ice to contend with. To keep the more irrationally ambitious crews from choosing that route in the interest of finding even more wind, the race committee had set a southern boundary. The crew had seen a couple of large bergs several miles off to starboard, but nothing closer. A bow watch for growlers was on constant, one-hour shifts, and nothing had been spotted. But they all knew sustaining speeds of around twenty knots day after day had to be putting a nasty strain on boat and gear.

The water never stopped flying, the boat's many voices never stopped shouting, laughing, hollering, and screaming as it planed down fifteen-to-twenty-foot waves, slammed into rogue seas, and kept trying to take scary knockdowns. The work never stopped. The helmsmen held everyone's well-being in their hands. After an hour at the helm they were toast, such was the effort to keep *All American* upright and in the groove, both safe and fast.

Rigging was routinely checked. Places where chafe could occur were frequently examined. Jib sheets had been changed several times. Many days of being constantly redlined had a certain numbing effect on the crew. One can imagine the thrill of hitting twenty-plus knots on a sixty-footer for a few hours. After days of it, the routine of being constantly soaked and cold, struggling to stay upright on the deck, trying to get any sleep as the boat surged and slammed, and the ordeal of pumping one's personal bilge in the midst of all that, became torturous.

The racket the boat made as it tore its way over and through the seas was extraordinary. Down below might have been a high-volume echo chamber for a sound-effects disc of car crashes and construction sites. It took a while to comprehend that a sudden violent sound did not necessarily mean something had broken or been damaged. But there was always the chance that it did.

Every sailor on board harbored unspoken anxiety about the boat's ability to handle such extreme, sustained conditions. Crewmen off watch collapsed below on sail bags in their foulies. If they were needed on deck there would be no time to dress. "My uncle," Dave Zimmer said to Sargent as he spooned another glop of freeze-dried mystery "food" into his mouth during a meal grabbed while sitting on wet sail bags, "was a fighter pilot. Nam. He could fall asleep anywhere if he had ten minutes because that's how uncertain it was between missions. That horn would go off, and they'd scramble. As a kid I never quite understood. Now I get it."

Sargent related how a doctor had done a sleep study with a solo round-the-world sailor. "His autopilot went out on him and he had to steer for almost thirty hours in big following seas. He told the doc he went into some stage of sleep for three to four seconds when he was planing down the face of a wave, and would wake up when he was sailing up the back of the next one. The doc said that had probably saved him."

Fifty miles from Cape Horn, the Low that had carried them ran out of gas. The afterguard (Damaris, Jan Sargent, and Andy) had been slowly aiming the boat further north, by all accounts the most favorable approach to Cape Horn. When the sun had risen on their fourteenth day out of Auckland, there it was, the stubby profile of

Cape Horn. Rising less than a thousand feet, Cape Horn is an inconsequential peak among South America's many giants. What it lacks in physical stature, it makes up for in designating a world-famous land's end. Some of the roughest seas in the world can be found there, along with the gales that help create them. Drake Passage, between Cape Horn and the Antarctic Peninsula, is where the Southern Ocean is at its narrowest. As it approaches the Cape, the ocean bottom rises from ten thousand feet to a few hundred feet in just a few miles, a steep profile that creates mountainous seas. But not this day.

"More good luck," Sargent said quietly, training his binoculars on Cape Horn. The sun was out, the sky was clear. It was blowing eight to ten knots. The boat was quiet, plodding along at the speed of the wind. The crew had organized the boat. It was drying out below. Everyone was up, not wanting to miss this magic moment.

"This is Cape Horn? Where's all the heroics, man?" It was Larry Kolegeri, obviously unimpressed.

"I'll take it," Damaris said. "You wanna see muscle? Watch the videos. There are plenty. The best one was shot by a guy named Irving Johnson in nineteen thirty. Famous sailor and storyteller. He had one of the first movie cameras, eight millimeter. Amazing dude. Climbed to the topm'st of the four-hundred-foot schooner he was on and shot the waves, graybacks he called them, decks awash. They were in a hundred-fifty-mile-per-hour storm. Wrote a book about it."

"This is like going to watch the Jets play and discovering Joe Namath is out sick, if you know what I mean."

"We could leave you here in the RIB if you want the

experience," Sargent said. "I'm told there's a gale here every three or four days."

"All right," Larry said, "so I'll watch the videos."

An hour later, with Cape Horn abeam off to port, Sargent produced a bottle of vodka that was passed around. Some of it was dutifully poured into the sea as a gesture of respect for Neptune, one of Mother Nature's heavies.

Six hours later, sailing north up the coast of Argentina, they got hammered. They'd opted to sail inside the Falkland Islands, which lie about four hundred miles offshore, in hopes of picking up a more southerly slant to the wind. That had not worked out. The wind had stayed west, smack on the beam, and honking, with gusts over thirty. The main was reefed, and still the end of the boom was dragging in the water in the gusts. Stu was driving, and sailing deeper than he wanted to take the strain off the gear. The seas were also beam-on, and large. Finding a fast path through the waves was a challenge for the helmsman, a matter of coming off a bit to surf down the face of one wave and not getting smacked when he came up over the top of the next one. If he nailed it three waves out of every five he was racking up hall-of-fame points.

The mains'l ripped apart that night, fourteen hours after rounding Cape Horn. It took all hands nearly a half hour to wrestle the sail down, organize it on deck, and raise the storm trysail, which would at least provide some headway. "I hate to say it," Larry Kolegeri said to Damaris as they were fighting with the sail, struggling to pull the wet luff down out of the mast groove a few inches at a time, "it's crazy, but having this happen is a relief. I knew the Old Lady was screwing with us. It could have been the mast. I'll take this."

"Should have given her the whole bottle," Damaris said.

The brutal work began. Dick Hooper, who had re-placed RD, supervised the operation. He handed out sail needles, palms, and waxed thread. The main had ripped from the outer edge toward the mast about halfway up. The tear had increased to fifteen feet or more by the time the crew had gotten the sail down. The idea was for the men on deck to bring the torn edges together with patch material, tacking it together every four inches or so. The crew worked in pairs, one passing the needle through the sail, the other retrieving it on the other side and passing it back through. Then it was hauled below to Hooper, who would finish the job by wrestling it through the sewing machine. Those who weren't sewing sat on the sail to keep it from sliding into the sea, because while the reduction in boat speed had made the motion less violent, the spray less constant, the weather had not changed. Thanks to cold fingers trying to manipulate the heavy sail needles on an unsteady platform, the patches were soon liberally spotted with blood. The darkness didn't help. It was an exhausting, uncomfortable process.

The repair to the main took six hours, six hours when *All American*'s speed was reduced to eight knots; six hours when they knew the other boats were doing twice that, or more. The wind abated a bit as dawn broke, but getting the main back up was still a struggle. At the helm, Andy would bear off to get headway, then bring the boat close to the wind, at which point there would be lots of feeding of the luff rope into the mast groove and cranking of the halyard. After half a dozen repetitions, the sail was up, and trimmed.

"Looks pretty good," Dave Zimmer said, examining the patchwork.

"Looks to me like another case of rum," Sargent said. He was right. On the twenty-second day out of Auckland, when they had a good view of the finish line off Punta del Este, Uruguay, there was *Ram Bunctious* at the dock.

"I'm just glad to be here," Sargent said. "Glad I'm able to buy him a case of rum."

XIII

SONNY

The sound of hundreds of peepers, tree frogs, and beetles was a symphony gone mad in the dark Mustique night. The noise was penetrating, amazingly loud. It made thinking difficult, and at the moment Isha needed to think. She and Jodi were sitting in their Mule, which was poked into the underbrush at an uncomfortable angle. The steering had failed suddenly, and they had gone into the rough before Isha could hit the brakes. Neither of them was hurt. Isha had turned the thing off, and the two of them were suddenly bombarded by the racket coming from all sides that had been drowned out by the Mule's engine. It was after midnight. They were both feeling frazzled, having begun the night at a cocktail party and ended up back at Rosco's in the village. Now their comforting control of the night from the security of their trusty Mule was gone. In a remote part of the small island they were being serenaded by the voice of the humid Caribbean darkness that was very alive, and it felt slightly menacing.

"Now what?" Jodi said. "I can tell you it's a long walk, mostly uphill. I don't have the radio. Forgot it. Mark will be pissed. Screw Mark." She opened her bag, pulled out a joint, and lit it. Isha said nothing, and declined when Jodi offered it.

It struck Isha what a metro girl she was, how un-prepared she was for real life on an untamed landscape unless it was in a house with plumbing, a coffee maker, and doors that locked. She had to laugh at the notion of walking more than a hundred yards on the rock-strewn, potholed dirt road in the frail designer flats on her feet. And there was Jodi, sucking on another joint. Ahh, to be eighteen and zonked beyond giving a shit. "We wait," Isha said, "unless you have a better idea."

"Waiting sounds good. Don't you love those frogs? They're the high-pitched screamers. Listen . . . I love it! I chased one. It woke me up. I was pissed. Jumped out of bed stark naked and went looking for the little bug-ger. Found him. He was naked too. Almost white in my flashlight. Slick with goo. You know how big he was? Like this." Jodi held up her hand, with about an inch between her thumb and forefinger. "A little alien creature. All that racket from something this big. I didn't kill him. Couldn't. Just chased him away."

Fifteen minutes passed. A half hour. Jodi had nodded off. Isha was wide awake, eyes closed, with the symphony of night critters playing games in her head. She could hear everything from car crashes and fingernails on black-boards to bits of long-forgotten melodies, infants crying, and the staccato signature of a Mule motor. That one got louder. She opened her eyes and saw the headlights coming around the curve. She flicked on the Mule's lights.

The vehicle stopped beside them. "Whassup?"

Isha recognized Sonny. She shrugged. "Broken."

Jodi stirred. "It's Sonny. Hi, Sonny."

"Hop in."

When they arrived at Goliath House, Sonny cut the engine. Jodi stumbled out and headed for the guesthouse with a wave. "Night all. Thanks, Sonny, for saving us."

"Good you came along," Isha said to Sonny.

"That's my job, coming along. What's yours?"

"Being there."

"You're a worker bee, right? Creighton's worker bee, I would guess. Not a bad gig as gigs go."

"Thanks, Sonny," Isha said as she made to leave the Mule.

"Hey, we're just getting to know each other." Sonny's hand was light on Isha's shoulder, his fingers moving, enjoying the velvety smoothness of her skin. "You're new. This is my island. Ask me anything, go ahead. This is an island full of dark secrets because it's full of the filthy rich. And here's a secret: you don't get to be filthy rich unless you have a dark secret. Everyone here has one. Whaddaya wanna know? Ask me. Maybe I'll tell you . . . if I know." Sonny chuckled.

Isha looked at Sonny, so brash, so confident, such a Brooklyn bullshitter. Such a great act. She decided to play.

"All right," she said, her eyes on his. "The other night I overheard you talking with Jocko about smuggling, something about a package on a race boat."

"Yeah, that was something, no? On a race boat! You heard that? The walls have ears. Can't be too careful. Who are you, anyway?"

"Have you learned any more about that?"

"You're interested in smuggling?"

"Why not?"

"You a cop? Just kidding. That's cool. Arrest me. Please. Ha ha. You want a few details."

"I would."

"I'll put it on the list. Now, who are you?"

"Jodi's companion."

"I get a feeling you know RD, Mark's new skipper."

"We've met."

"Those," Sonny said, looking at Isha's chest, "are very impressive, I have to say. Must have cost a fortune."

"They did," Isha said, pulling back her shoulders for full effect and turning toward Sonny. "The lilies got gilded."

"But you didn't pay."

"That's my secret." Isha leaned over and gave Sonny a sisterly kiss on the cheek before she got out of the Mule. His hand briefly engaged one of her breasts in a way that could have been considered accidental. It wasn't. "Thanks for the lift," she said. Sonny started the Mule. His laugh and the motor noise became diminuendo in the critters' symphony as Sonny rolled down the driveway.

"I have to ask," Jodi said, "didn't I see you coming out of Mark's workout room earlier this afternoon?" Jodi and Isha were at the pool, enjoying some deviled eggs Tomas had brought them. "It's none of my business, but . . ."

"That's true, it's none of your business, but the answer is yes."

"Oh my God . . ." Jodi was smiling.

"It's just therapy. Physical therapy."

Jodi stared at Isha, then started laughing, losing some deviled egg into her hand. Isha laughed with her.

"I'd say that's on the extracurricular side," Jodi said, licking the egg off her hand, still laughing. "I hope there will be some, ah, additional . . ."

"Oh yes. And very generous additional, I must say."

"Worth every penny, I'm sure."

"Worth every penny." Both women had a good laugh.

Jodi lay back on the chaise, closed her eyes, and put on her sunglasses. Isha bit into another deviled egg.

"My father practiced physical therapy on me," Jodi said.

Isha listened.

"Good-night tuck-ins started getting a little too friendly. It progressed from there. When I was twelve he started coming in wearing just his bathrobe."

"I can relate."

"Really?"

"Pretty much the same, only mine was drunk. More like an attack."

"Not Daddy. Stone-cold sober. But an attack, still. A chip off Mark's block."

Jodi was quiet.

"What'd you do?" Isha asked.

"Nothing for a while. Too scared. He kept giving me money. Lots. And stuff. I liked that. When I was fourteen I realized I was a prostitute. So I began studying airplane mechanics. For his airplane. He had a large manual I found. Figured out how to make shit happen."

"It was you?"

"Yep."

"But your mother . . . ?"

"She wasn't supposed to be on the flight. But she knew. How could she not? She had to. Fuckers. Both of them."

Isha stared up at the frigate birds floating serenely on the invisible ocean of air. At least they looked serene. Who could tell. She could smell her father's foul liquor breath, feel his hands groping her. A wave of nausea wafted over her like a winter chill.

"What did you do?" Jodi asked.

"I left one night. I was sixteen. Took a backpack."

"Never went back?"

"This Christmas. First time. He came at me. I hit him with a ten-pound dumbbell."

"Whoa! Kill him?"

"Didn't stick around to find out."

They were quiet, lost for a moment in their own vengeance.

"Revenge is sweet," Jodi said.

"Yes it is." Isha paused. "I have such a project going right now, in fact."

"Really?"

"I could use some help. Interested?"

"Revenge? Are you kidding? Count me in."

Dinner was boiled lobsters flown in live from Maine.

Mark had sent his pilots, who had remained in Barbados with the aircraft, to get them that morning. Isha couldn't stand the idea of eating the large, bug-like creatures. Tomas had the cook fix her a piece of chicken. Mark was visibly disappointed.

XIV

KNIFE MAN

Andy was counting. With a sound that raised the goosebumps on one's neck and that could create anxiety even for the innocent, the fourth heavy metal gate slammed and locked shut irrevocably behind them as Andy and his attorney made their way into the bowels of INR Las Rosas prison in Punta del Este, Uruguay. The rank odor was powerful, a mixture of bad institutional food and bodies, lots of bodies penned up in windowless eight-by-ten enclosures. The innocent! Andy would have laughed if it had been appropriate, but a laugh in this place, where the guards all wore permanent hostile faces, would have probably been considered a criminal act. And those guards held the keys to his departure. If the little can in the keel of *All American* were found here in Punta, could he end up in Las Rosas? More goosebumps.

The sound of drilling. A repair was going on. Andy stared at the men working, drilling into metal. It took him back on the boat, with Martin sweating like a pig under the sound-suppressing blanket, drilling for what seemed an eternity into the boat's keel, the sound echoing into the harbor and being carried for miles by the water to anyone who happened to be listening; and Grady biting into another shrimp with that confounding, blank-faced confidence of his, talk about innocence, washing it down with another shot of Don Julio, asking quietly for Andy's assurance . . . His father, for chrissakes, his father, found after damn near thirty years, such a cool dude, so respected by everyone, his father asking for his assurance. What was he supposed to say? No? Sorry, Dad, your son can't handle it. Maybe. Probably. And Becky's "How could you?!" How could he. How could he not?

"Mr. Moss . . . Sir!"

Andy pulled himself out of it. The attorney he had hired as a translator was trying to get his attention. They had arrived. No more metal gates. "Visitantes" was imprinted on a door one of the guards was holding open for them. They walked into a sizable room with bars on the high windows and were seated at one of the metal tables that, along with the chairs, had been screwed into the floor. They waited. An armed guard waited with them.

Knife Man was almost impossible to recognize without his braid, with his scruffy but sanitary prison haircut. A guard brought him in and seated him at the table across from Andy and the attorney. He was larger than Andy remembered. But it was him. The eyes had it.

Andy had gotten to look straight into those eyes after the man had first knocked him to the ground, when abject fear had not yet been replaced by the violent surge of anger he hadn't known he had in him. Perez was his name. Antonio Perez. He had been cooperative, providing evidence that would have locked Mitchell Thomas away for a long time even without the murder conviction for Andy's mother's death; evidence that would have nailed Isha as well if she hadn't slipped away. For that, Perez had been given a light sentence (for Uruguay) of five years. Attempted murder had been reduced to assault with a deadly weapon. Sam had made it all happen with the attorney Andy had contacted.

The attorney, Jaime Mejia, knew Perez. He asked him, in Spanish, how he was doing. Perez shrugged. Then he looked at Andy and shook his head. He spoke in Spanish to Mejia, ending his comment with a little chuckle.

"He says he still can't understand how he got beat by a punk like you," Mejia said to Andy.

Andy smiled at Perez. "I only have one question. I need to know if the woman who made the deal with him, the woman who paid him, wanted him to kill me."

Mejia translated. Perez looked daggers at Andy.

"The wooman," Perez said in English. He laughed and held his hands, cupped, palms facing in, in front of his chest. "The wooman, ha ha ha. Oh yes. Kill. Yes, she say kill." And he went on, talking a blue streak in Spanish and laughing some more, while dragging his index finger across his throat.

Driving back to the hotel, Andy asked Mejia what Perez's long diatribe in Spanish had been about. "It was very colorful," Mejia said. "But the gist of it was how you must have been lousy in bed."

✳

Both Sargent and Joe Dugan thought that was extremely funny. Andy was filling them in over a few pints, since they were the ones who had happened along and had probably stopped him from killing Perez the night he'd attacked Andy.

"A woman scorned!" Sargent said.

"Such bullshit," Andy said. "In those days I was a fool, drunk a lot of the time, stoned, and she portioned it out like it was a World Series ticket with a locker-room pass."

"Look, but don't touch," Dugan said.

"Touch, but not much," Sargent said, and the two men had a good laugh.

"Yeah, and who do you think paid for those things?"

"I do remember that night, when we got back to your hotel room and I bandaged your arm," Dugan said, "and she came in, saw us there, got pissed, and then — then she saw you. I won't forget the look on her face. Whopping surprise for sure. But immense relief, immense regret? Who could tell? Maybe both."

"Now we know," Andy said.

"You can't be sure," Sargent said. "You gonna believe a killer for hire serving five years who is still embarrassed he got beat by a gringo? A guy who wants to make it hot for you?"

Sargent ordered three more pints.

"Why'd you go to all that trouble, getting an attorney, doing all that paperwork, to see Perez?" Dugan wondered. "Why bother. You know what a weird piece of work Isha was . . . is."

Andy studied his beer. "Is. Unfinished business, I guess. She's out there. I know her. I know I haven't seen the last of her. I needed to know if she just rides shotgun, or if she could pull the trigger."

XV

CRUISING

It could have been worse.

After that lobster dinner, the Creightons, Jodi, and Isha had adjourned to the open-air garden built into the middle of the house on Mustique. The garden was ablaze with flowers and large native plants and included a meandering pool of decorative carp. RD, *Orion*'s captain, joined them to propose a plan for a cruise. He had outlined a two-week round trip north from Mustique, with stops in Saint Lucia, Martinique, and Dominica. Mark Creighton was delighted with the plan, but his wife, Nancy, dismissed it out of hand, citing Jodi's lack of enthusiasm for sailing, what would be Nina's first time cruising, and her own obligations on the island. Mark didn't even bother to protest, as Nancy pointed out that for such an extended voyage as RD suggested, Mark could surely find a few other old salts who shared his inane desire "to go to sea." A fearsome intimidator in business, Mark knew when not to force an issue with his wife.

RD had quickly come up with a three-day cruise to Saint Lucia, a mere sixty miles north, a comfortable day sail for *Orion*. Nancy thought that would be very nice. Isha dreaded the thought of any of it, but knew there was no way out. RD had provided Isha with the latest acupressure bracelet along with some reliable pills to combat seasickness. It was a good thing, because it blew fifteen to twenty knots out of the east the day they sailed to Saint Lucia. Under reefed main and a small jib, it was a rolling beam reach that let the old yawl show what it could do. It was a joy to those familiar with sailing offshore, but for a novice, even for Jodi and Nancy, it was on the wild side, as the boat's speedo frequently hit double figures, heaving thick bow waves to either side as it powered down the fronts of large seas. Every so often an out-of-sequence wave would smack the hull broadside, causing anxiety for those unaccustomed to knowing when to hang on. Isha watched the salt spray drying white on her arms and legs.

The sail took about six hours. RD had cautioned Isha to stay on deck in the fresh air rather than try to deal with the unexpected jolts and the stuffy conditions below that could cause nasty bruises as well as mal de mer. He showed her a safe place to sit, wedged in the cockpit. After an hour or so, given the boat's consistently stable behavior and the obvious enjoyment being exhibited by RD, his crew, and Mark Creighton, she started to relax. The bracelet and pills seemed to be working, the sun was warm, the boat seemed equal to the task. She began to appreciate the remarkable experience she was having. Sailing! This gorgeous boat was stretched out before her, the sails full, turning the water to hissing foam with its powerful passage, the deck wet and glistening, the lines taut, and all the new sounds of water and wind. This was one for the memory book. If it didn't kill her. Isha Mowbry was sailing! How . . . fancy! "Dolphins under the bow!" Mark called out, causing Jodi to run forward. Isha could see them jumping. Amazing! She'd have to tell Cameron.

She was also very glad when they sailed into the lee of Saint Lucia and things calmed down. Soon sails were doused, and under power they were turning into an anchorage on the west coast, flanked by two very tall, striking pitons and fronted by a lovely beach and a handsome hotel, where Nancy announced they had reservations. "The crew needs to pick up," Nancy said. "I like my bath hot and deep, thank you very much. And the food there is simply marvelous."

The next day, Nancy had arranged to play tennis, and Mark was off skin diving, freeing Jodi and Isha to rent motor scooters and announce they would tour the island. Their real mission was to find Captain Jerome, an uncle of their friend Rosco on Mustique. They had told Rosco what Jocko, the diamond king, had said about smuggling. When he heard they were off to Saint Lucia, Rosco told them they had to find his uncle, who might know more. That was all he would say. But he said he'd be in touch with the captain, let him know they might be coming around. He drew them a little map of how to find him.

Isha and Jodi's first stop on Rosco's map was to find a fellow with the unlikely name of Sunshine Biscuit. The two of them, Rosco had told them with a smile, needed a guide who would protect them from the more ambitious dudes who would be competing to show them around. The Biscuit, he said, could be found in a village not far from where they would come ashore. He said Biscuit was good friends with the captain, and people didn't mess with him.

They found Biscuit on a narrow, steep little street full of tiny dwellings nestled side by side, carving the fish and birds he sold to tourists. He was expecting them, but Rosco had obviously not mentioned the beauty that would be appearing before him. They had dressed down for the occasion, but even so, for a moment the two striking women brought a stop to neighborhood activity. Biscuit was a powerfully built man. His eyes registered surprise and appreciation while his demeanor remained low-key and polite. He immediately invited them into his home, where he offered them cans of soda and something to smoke. Isha and Jodi could barely process how sparely he lived, or how Biscuit's tiny "bedroom" was consumed by two stereo speakers bigger than steamer trunks. Together the speakers were larger than his cot. "Yes," he said, "got to have music." Jodi couldn't resist asking him about his name. "The brand for my carvings," he said with a smile. "Hard to forget." Indeed.

Biscuit had his own scooter, a gift from the captain, he said, and soon the women were following him on trails that became ever narrower as they led deeper into the bush.

The captain's hideaway in a clearing was impressive. The rhythmic wash of a small, nearby waterfall that produced the clear stream sliding past his dwelling was constant, a sound like wind in the trees. The house was grand by comparison to how other Saint Lucians lived, but still simple, built of local materials and designed to serve basic needs. It looked as if it had grown in place. Biscuit stopped a respectable distance from the house, where the three visitors were greeted by two imposing young Saint Lucian men with machetes hanging from their belts. Isha spotted a few others lounging around nearby. Guards? she wondered. They greeted Biscuit as one of their own, and they were friendly to Jodi and Isha. Nearby, in an open structure with a thatched roof of palm fronds, three women were tie-dyeing fabric. Their colorful work was drying in the sun.

Captain Jerome was a surprise. Both Isha and Jodi later agreed they had expected someone much older. Jerome was a Saint Lucian native, but taller than most, and fit. Like the other men, he was dressed in shorts, but his top was a faded polo shirt bearing a yacht's name with two crossed burgees embroidered over one breast. His full shock of hair was very white, providing a certain dignity. Isha didn't think he could be a day over fifty. He spoke French patois with his fellows, but his English was excellent, colored by an intriguing accent. He gave Biscuit a powerful hug. Soon the four of them were seated in a comfortable glade, enjoying glasses of cold tea.

"So you are hanging out with Rosco over on Mustique," Jerome said. "Be careful. He is a dangerous boy." Jerome shook his head and chuckled.

"You are his uncle?" Jodi asked.

"Something like that. I understand you are Mark Creighton's granddaughter. Mr. Creighton, the big boss who got rich poisoning our planet, and you have arrived here on *Orion*, the lovely Sparkman and Stephens yawl from the late nineteen thirties."

"You know about my grandfather, and his boat."

"Oh yes. We have power here," he chuckled. "My laptop tells me everything. And local communications are very good. I have another nephew who runs the waterfront at the hotel where you stayed last night. But you" — Jerome turned to Isha — "you are a bit of a mystery. Rosco said it is you who has the questions. And who might you be, if I might ask?"

"I am Nina," Isha said, "Nina Simpson. I am Jodi's companion."

"It is a nice name," Jerome said, "but common. A companion? No story. Is there a story? There must be a story."

"I could ask you the same thing," Isha said. "Jerome. Captain Jerome. Jerome who? There must be a story there."

Jerome scratched his head, sipped his tea. "Jerome Butler. I'm a private man," he said. "Having seen much of it, I prefer to keep the outside world at arm's length. But perhaps we could have an exchange. If you would agree to respect my privacy, I could tell you a little about me. Then you could tell me a little about you."

"I would agree to that, if you also respect my privacy," Isha said.

Jerome grinned. "I grew up here in Saint Lucia," he said. "Learned the water, fishing, sailing. Had a hotel job when I was seventeen. Ran the small rental boats. Got friendly with people who sailed in on a maxi. They liked the way I did things, offered me a job. I took it. Sailed away for fifteen years. Worked on many yachts. Learned the game. Became a captain. Had some good adventures, then enough was enough. Missed being home. Came back. That's the short version."

"I grew up in the Bronx," Isha said, "New York, tough neighborhood. My father, a drunk, repeatedly attacked me when I was a teenager. One night when I was sixteen, I left, for good. I've been living by my wits ever since. I've had some good times, and some bad times that were near misses with the law."

"Well, that's pretty good," Jerome said, smiling, taking a joint out of a dish on the table and striking a large wooden match. "Please help yourselves to some of the best weed in the world, grown right here in Saint Lucia. Piton Pure, we call it."

Jodi helped herself. "We'll share," she said to Jerome, indicating Isha. Biscuit helped himself.

"You seem very comfortable here," Isha said.

"I did well on the boats," Jerome said.

"You seem to spread the wealth. That's friendly. People must be grateful."

"Here on Saint Lucia life is pretty easy. A little goes a long way."

"It looks like more than a little. You must have been a very good saver. Or maybe you got lucky?"

Jerome took a drag and exhaled a cloud of smoke. "Are you living by your wits right now, Nina?" he asked with a gracious smile. Biscuit gave a low chuckle.

Jodi had passed Nina the joint. "I am," she said with a laugh as she contributed a cloud of smoke to the conversation. Jerome laughed at her. Mostly he was laughing at himself. This little package of dynamite was taking him back to his years fraternizing in some of the most prestigious yacht clubs in the world, witnessing that lavish culture — being part of it as a professional — learning how to play in that high-end, not-much-matters society where anything goes as long as it's dressed right. It had been ten years since he'd made his six-figure score with the diamonds. It had been easy using the maxi he was captain of, with its billionaire owner no one was going to bother. No one. A guy like Creighton. Ten years ago. Done. Back home. Squeaky clean. And now here comes this babe with her questions. My oh my.

"What are you getting at?" Jerome asked her.

"A fellow we met on Mustique is a high roller in the diamond business. We heard him talking about smuggling, about how he plays both sides. He said something about using sailboats as carriers. Race boats. Have you heard of such a thing?"

"I might have," Jerome said.

"Think it is still going on?"

Jerome laughed. "Could be."

"I know nothing about boats. I have so many questions. Where would you hide such a . . . package . . . on a boat?"

Jerome studied the sky. "Are you planning to become a smuggler?"

"It's not a bad idea, really." Isha paused. She knew it was time to show a few cards. Jerome would tell her some things, she was sure. But she had to play. Jodi passed her the joint. She took another hit. Jerome was right. It was very good. Piton Pure seemed to provide enhanced perspective, establish priorities, eliminate bothersome details, and cut to the chase. The white noise of the waterfall provided a reassuring soundtrack. The row of tie-dyed garments hanging in the sun was a heady blaze of color bringing a certain whimsy to the weight of the bush. Birds spoke sharply as they flew their speedy forays. The world seemed in sync here in this bountiful hideaway of Jerome's. Isha felt secure.

"Revenge," Isha said. "That's my mission. People have something that belongs to me. I want it back. Simple." She shrugged.

"Ahh, revenge," Jerome said. "A strong beast, that one. He can get his claws into you."

"I know. I know," she said with a sly smile. "But the satisfaction!"

Jerome's smile was indulgent. "The package, to start with," he said, "is usually not very big, making it fairly easy to hide. With this in mind, study *Orion* when you get back aboard. Imagine you need to hide something less than half the size of a can of tennis balls. So many places. The spars: masts, booms, spinnaker poles. The rigging, the spreaders. Inside the winches. In the keel." Jerome paused. "I've heard of holes being drilled in the keel bulb, but retrieval becomes a problem. Too public. The boat must be hauled. One group, Australians I think, was fond of removing a keel bolt. Quick and easy once they got the hang of it."

"Australians."

"I'm quite sure it was Australians."

When it was time to leave, Jodi asked Jerome if he might have some Piton Pure he would part with. "I would be happy to make a purchase."

"Of course," he said, nodding to one of his ma-chete-wearing friends, who disappeared and returned quickly with a little parcel. "Please accept this with my compliments," he told Jodi.

"No, really," she said. "I would be happy to . . ."

"Please. I insist," Jerome said.

They sailed back to Mustique on one of those gor-geous, sun-slick Caribbean days when the wind is light and the seas are calm. RD's crew raised the mainsail and a sizable jib and turned on the engine. The result was a relaxed, comfortable passage.

Isha and Jodi made their way to the foredeck, where they could talk without being heard. RD and the Creigh-tons were sitting in the cockpit. The crew was busy doing boat work and making lunch. Jodi had questions. Isha's focus on the smuggling bit had caught her attention. She was eager to know more. Jodi's curiosity was exactly what Isha wanted. "Eager" created a useful avenue for disinfor-mation. Isha had worked on her story, craftily coloring a few facts for Jodi's young ears.

"His name is Andy," Isha told Jodi. "Wealthy. We were engaged. I was his partner in a development project, a theme-park-type hotel based on astronomy, his hobby. He dumped me, which wasn't so bad. He was a bore, ac-tually. What hurt was that he cut me out of the project. His lawyers made me disappear. I had money invested. All gone."

"Couldn't you sue him?"

"Impossible with his army of lawyers. I didn't have a chance. Plus I was out of money."

"They could have at least paid you off."

"At least."

"But where does the smuggling come in?"

"Andy is on a boat in that yacht race around the world. Maybe you've heard of it? The Race."

Jodi shook her head.

"The boats just left Uruguay for Fort Lauderdale. You heard what Jocko told Sonny. You heard what Jerome said. It's starting to add up. I'm not sure why, I just have a strong sense that Andy is involved."

"And if he is . . ."

"Exactly. We need to relieve him of the package."

"How do we do that?" Jodi's "we" was not lost on Isha.

"RD has lots of friends in Fort Lauderdale. He'll be stopping there taking this boat back to Connecticut."

"We fly home next week. We could meet him there."

"We need more information. And money."

"Money is not a problem," Jodi said.

Isha's work with Jodi had paid off, literally. And she didn't have long to wait long for the information. The cocktail party the evening after they returned to Mustique was at Sonny's. Isha and Jodi hadn't been there fifteen minutes before Sonny found them. "Look at you two," Sonny said quietly. "Does it get any better?" He hugged Jodi, kissed her on the cheek. "I hope I won't be arrested. You're eighteen, right?" Sonny chuckled as he put an arm around Isha's waist. "Excuse us, okay?" he said to Jodi. "Nina and I have some business."

Sonny ushered Isha along a narrow, twisting path down a hill toward the ocean, where the swimming pool was located. They went into the pool house, with its comfortable little living room and bar, open to the sea. Sonny's staff had lit a few candles at his request.

"Here we are," Sonny said. He went to the bar and poured two glasses of champagne from a bottle nestled in ice, handed one to Isha. He touched his glass to hers. They drank. "I think I have something for you," Sonny said.

"Really?"

"Something you were asking about."

"Really."

"Yeah. But first, you have a little something for me."

"I do?"

"'You can leave your hat on.'"

"What?"

"You don't know that?" Sonny gave her a half smile, his eyes questioning. "Randy Newman song. Joe Cocker made it famous. Nineteen eighty-six, it came out." Sonny half sang the lyrics: "'Baby, take off your dress, yes, yes, yes.' I was there, in the studio. Two takes, that's all. Two takes! Joe was amazing. Freaking Joe." Sonny shook his head, poured more champagne.

"One of the great moments in music. Perfect song. Randy and Joe." Sonny again half sang the lyrics: "'Stand on that chair, raise your arms up in the air, and now shake 'em . . .' But you can leave your hat on. God, how I love it. I was there. Now I'm here. Fantastic. Isn't it?" He stared at her.

Isha stared back. She put her glass down without her eyes leaving Sonny's. Slowly, starting at the top, she began unbuttoning her light cotton top. With a deft little shrug she slipped it off her shoulders to the floor. Then, slowly, she raised her arms, entwined her fingers, and gave a little shake.

Sonny was beyond enchanted. Again, he half sang the lyrics as he feasted on the beauty: "'You give me reason to live, you give me reason to live, you give me reason to live.'" He took a step and embraced Isha.

After a long moment, Isha slowly and artfully disengaged herself. She picked up her top with one hand, her glass of champagne with the other. "Your turn," she said, taking a sip.

"It's a name," Sonny said, working to regain his composure. "It took some persuading. I got it from Jocko, told him I wanted in."

"Yes?"

"Grady. That's it. Just . . . Grady."

"Thank you, Sonny."

"No," Sonny said quietly. "Thank you."

XVI

DOLDRUMS

Andy figured the leg from Punta to Miami had to have been designed by sadists to test sailors' sanity. If the Southern Ocean had tried their stamina, their endurance, and had severely challenged every crewman's ability as a seaman, the 7,000 miles from Punta to the States promised a bout with light and variable conditions highlighted by the dreaded Doldrums, situated in the Convergence Zone, where the weather systems of the northern and southern hemispheres merge at the equator. The result is a band of breathless calms cluttered with huge puddles of seaweed and other flotsam that can further inhibit headway. Samuel Taylor Coleridge's poem *The Rime of the Ancient Mariner*, a tale of dehydration and starvation caused by a mariner's thoughtless killing of a friendly albatross, is presumed to be set in the Doldrums. Becalmed under a blazing sun for many days, the mariner and his hapless mates were, Coleridge wrote, "as idle as a painted ship upon a painted ocean."

Sargent, Damaris, and Andy had spent hours ashore before the start looking at weather patterns for March and April going back twenty years and consulting with meteorologists about current influences. Their hope was to pick a spot in that thousand-mile expanse of limbo where they might find a breeze that would carry them through. They knew it was a very long shot. Luck would be a considerable factor.

They had done well on the 2,800-mile section from Punta del Este to Recife, a city on the tip of the elbow Brazil extends into the Atlantic. They had stayed one hundred fifty miles or so offshore, enough to avoid the erratic behavior of the easterlies as they approached the coast, but not so far east as to fall into the recurring mid-Southern Atlantic Low between Brazil and Africa's west coast. Recife had been off the port beam after sixteen days of sailing. Not bad. "I drove Punta to Recife once," Sargent had told his crew. "Took me seventy hours." And still they kept moving well, crossing the equator on day seventeen, with the Amazon basin abeam to the west. It wasn't for almost three hundred more miles that they came to a halt — a painted ship upon a painted ocean.

After more than nineteen days afloat, with the finish line in Miami still 3,000 miles distant, encountering the Doldrums was like running into stopped traffic on the New Jersey Turnpike on a hot summer day with the air-conditioning struggling and a couple of grumpy toddlers in the back seat. There wasn't much to do about it, or say. For several hours it was quiet on the boat as the sailors retreated into themselves, taking naps and organizing their spaces in between hoisting the largest, lightest headsail they had. After a while that was lowered to the deck rather than letting it flap about. The main was also lowered and flaked on the boom. Having it snapping above the crew's heads as the boat rolled in the gentle swells was just adding fuel to the frustration. Normally the main would be left up in a calm to catch whatever zephyrs happened along. But there were no zephyrs. The speedo was stuck on zero.

"I mean, this is flat!" Stu exclaimed, breaking the silence after several hours. "I've never seen anything quite like it. Flat! And we're in the middle of the Atlantic Ocean, hundreds of miles offshore, thousands of miles from Africa, and we're in the deadest, flattest calm I've ever seen! And I've raced on Long Island Sound! Come on . . . what the hell!"

Angry cursing was heard below deck. It was Larry Kolegeri. A few minutes later Larry's head appeared in the hatch. "Has anyone," he said in a voice that could have stopped a bear, "seen my boot?"

"Would that be the right or the left boot, Larry?" It was Joe Dugan, the smallest sailor on the boat, casually making light of the situation.

Larry glared at him. "It would be the right boot, Joe, not that it fucking matters which goddamn boot it is. They were in the useless goddamn drying locker, and now one of them is not there."

"Think someone took it?" It was Eric Menici.

"I dunno," Larry said, with a dangerous smile. "What size feet do you have, wiseass?"

"It must be in the locker if that's where you put it," Stu said.

"Maybe you'd like to come down here and have a look, Stu," Larry said, his anger building. "I'd be glad to stuff your ass in there so you could have a really good look."

"Calm down, Larry. Calm down for chrissakes. The boot will turn up. We'll find it." Sargent, down below, was trying to forestall trouble.

"Yeah, calm down, bro," Larry's brother, Caskie, chimed in from on deck. "I mean, it's not like you need boots right now, man. Or maybe you do, I dunno. It's only ninety-four degrees. Boots might be a good call. Myself, I'd prefer more sunscreen. Or maybe a cold beer."

Larry came out of the hatch and made his way through the cockpit to the mid-deck where Caskie was sitting. People moved out of his way. Caskie quickly stood up. This wasn't the first time his big brother had run amok.

"You take my boot, bro?" Larry asked. The two line-backers were face to face.

"What if I did?" Caskie said.

The two came together with a dull smack, both struggling to take the other down. The crew was silent. Sargent, who had rushed on deck, said quietly, "Okay, knock it off. Right now!" It was too late. As one tangled mass of muscle, the two lost their balance and went overboard. They came up still grappling. Sargent shook his head.

"Shark!" Stu yelled. "Shark!"

The two broke it off and sprinted for the boat. Crewmen grabbed their arms and shoulders and pulled them on board. Sputtering, Larry Kolegeri wiped his eyes, scanning the water. "No shark, right?"

"I swear I saw one," Stu said.

Larry started laughing. "Man, that felt good." He looked at Sargent. "Sorry."

"I didn't realize it was fourth and one," Sargent said.

Larry laughed again, then stood up and dove back in. One by one the rest of the crew followed until only Sargent was left on the boat. "It's all yours from here," Andy shouted at him.

"Screw you," Sargent muttered, securing the rope boarding ladder to the rail. Then he dove in.

It was a full twenty-four hours before a breath of wind stirred the masthead fly. It was night, but Andy's watch was on the case. Up went the big code-zero heads'l that had been flaked on deck. A very light sheet had already been attached. The sail was trimmed with care by hand and actually assumed some shape before the main was hauled up. Andy watched the speed gauge actually registering some headway — .5, 1, 1.5 knots. There were several more little zephyrs that brushed the sails, with the calm periods between them getting shorter and shorter until *All American* was ghosting along at between two and three knots. In the wrong direction. At least they were moving. Andy's fingertips were ever so light on the big wheel, teasing the boat toward the north as he felt the breeze trending ever so slightly right, moving due east as the minutes passed. They sailed several hours like this, with Damaris confident they were on the right track. "The easterly is a good sign," he assured Andy. "It should keep strengthening on this course."

He was right. In six hours the code zero had been replaced by the number one jib, and the speedo was steady on eight knots. The mood on the boat had improved noticeably. Larry had found his boot and mumbled apologies all around. No one had accepted them.

The easterly had strengthened enough so that in another day the afterguard was faced with the decision of how to best handle the approach to Miami. That decision had been the subject of a long discussion between Sargent, Andy, Damaris, and Stu several days before the start. The default course was to leave the Caribbean islands — from Grenada near South America to the Bahamas off Florida — to port, then turn left through the Bahamas into Miami. Damaris had broached another idea. "If the easterly trades seem locked in," he had argued, "we could sail into the Caribbean Sea, leave all those islands to starboard until we get to Puerto Rico, then cut back into the Atlantic between Puerto Rico's west end and the Dominican Republic. We'd have a faster, deeper wind angle instead of fighting a tighter reach all the way. And it's actually a shorter distance."

"How much deeper?" Andy asked.

"Ten degrees. At least. Maybe fifteen."

"Worth a few knots," Sargent said.

"Yep. Spinnaker maybe."

"How wide is that passage off Puerto Rico?" Sargent wanted to know.

"Hundred miles," Damaris said.

"Isn't there a little island in the middle?"

"Yeah, Mona Island. About five miles wide. Unoccupied."

"Wildlife sanctuary," said Stu. "Man, how I'd love to stop there. But, guys, that's Mona Passage, very tricky place, very close to the Puerto Rico Trench that's five miles deep. Deepest trench in the Atlantic. It depends on tides, and weather patterns, but Mona can kick ass. Wild thunderstorms, confused seas. Boats have been beat up going through Mona. Cruising boats sometimes wait weeks for a friendly weather window."

"Could be nasty at night," Sargent said.

"Actually it's supposed to ease off at night when the land cools."

"There's a lighthouse, Mona Island Light, east side, right where we want it," Damaris said.

"Puerto Rico could block an easterly wind," Andy said.

"Puerto Rico lays dead east and west," Damaris said. "I figure we'll slow down a little for maybe as much as ten miles running the cut. But it wouldn't be that bad if the easterly holds. We'd give the Puerto Rico side the widest possible berth."

"You'd be asking a lot," Sargent said. "We'd have to decide inside or outside at least twenty-four hours before we got there, and hope the easterly would hold."

"What about the other side?" Stu had asked. "The east end of Puerto Rico, Saint Croix side. I've been through there. Culebra Island is smack in the middle of that passage, lot of bars and rocks, but at night the whole place is lit up like a stadium."

"We'd have to sail higher to get there," Damaris said. "May as well stay outside. Puerto Rico is a hundred miles long. The whole idea is to stay deeper and faster."

Andy said he figured that Koonce would be going outside. "Don't we all agree?"

"Yes," Sargent had said. "Common knowledge is, only fools go inside. Every one of those islands is a blocker in an easterly."

"Not if you stay fifty to sixty miles away from them," Damaris said.

"Risks are part of this game," Andy said. "Knowing when to take them . . ."

"Remember Hen and Chickens," Sargent said, momentarily tempering the enthusiasm as they all replayed making a call on the way to Auckland that hadn't exactly turned out well. *Ram Bunctious* had made up a mile on them and drawn even, setting up a wild finish.

"You still got your case of rum," Andy said.

Sargent: "Yes I did."

The discussion had ended with three plans on the table. Plan A was going outside, referred to as the Koonce route, leaving the islands to port. Plan B was going inside, through the Caribbean Sea if the easterly trades were locked in, and using Mona Passage to get back into the Atlantic. Plan C was also inside, cutting back into the Atlantic at Culebra. But that was considered a backup in case it looked like Mona was having a tantrum.

Damaris had established a GPS point on the chart where a decision had to be made about which route they would take. It was very far out, three hundred miles from Grenada. But if they were to go the Koonce route, that was where they would have to start steering a little higher, more northerly. Given how the easterly had strengthened, Damaris's point of no return was coming up fast. The decision was made difficult by what they didn't know, like where *Ram Bunctious* was, or how badly — or favorably — their rival had been affected by the Doldrums.

Andy was enthusiastic about Damaris's Plan B. One had to assume that *Ram Bunctious* had done well in the Doldrums, better than they had done, and that their job was to catch them. Risk was part of racing, and, as he had argued, as far as risk was concerned, Plan B wasn't very extreme. Mona Passage might be tough, but it wasn't Cape Horn by any means.

Damaris went over the weather one last time as *All American* approached the GPS point he had named Helen, after an old girlfriend. The easterly was holding, looking good for a couple of days. Sargent wasn't totally sold on Plan B, but he ended up yielding to Damaris and Andy. With one condition. If *Ram* beat them by taking the Koonce route, they would buy the rum. Andy argued they should split it three ways. Done deal.

GPS Helen (8.11 degrees north, 52.7 degrees west) was roughly one hundred fifty miles north of French Guiana. When they had made Helen, they set a course to Mona Passage that would take them close by the northeast side of Grenada, a course that improved their wind angle by five degrees. With the wind blowing less than twenty knots, sometimes, the combination of course and wind speed allowed Sargent to call for the small asymmetrical spinnaker. Carrying it was a bit of a struggle, but it added two knots of boat speed. After the long haul up the South American coast, and the many grim hours in the Doldrums, the creative move to sail through the Caribbean had refocused the crew. They were cranked, ready to make the most of it.

✳

It had gotten dark when *All American* lined up Mona Passage. They had flown through the Caribbean. The easterly had stayed strong, and the course from Grenada to Mona had kept them away from the closest islands. As Damaris had figured, the deeper wind angle had allowed them to keep the spinnaker up and pulling for the twenty-four hours it had taken them to sail the four hundred miles. The Isla de Mona Light on the island's southeast side had come into view around 10:00 p.m., meaning they were fifteen miles out.

The current was with them, normally a good sign. But the water depth went from 25,000 feet to 2,000 feet in just fifty miles, a fact Damaris hadn't bothered to mention when he proposed Plan B. No sense getting everyone excited. The ocean floor had the same profile coming from the other direction. Imagine a very slender mountain four miles high — a massive, submarine piton — topping out a couple of thousand feet under the surface, its peak located in mid-Mona Passage. Such a radical contour could create some nasty waves if wind and current were right. Damaris hoped no north had developed in the easterly wind on the Atlantic side of Puerto Rico that would cause a wind-against-tide situation, creating brutal wave action known as "rooftops."

They were giving Puerto Rico the widest berth possible, cutting Mona Light as close as they dared, in hopes of staying out of the lee created by the large island. Still, they had slowed noticeably. "Not good," Sargent said as he watched the speedo drop to ten knots.

"The passage is more quiet at night, don't forget,"

Damaris reminded him. Sargent quietly cursed.

As *All American* approached Mona Island, the seas began to build into a confusing chop. With the wind speed down, the boat gave up its control to the seas that seemed to come from every direction, knocking the crew about mercilessly. Stu was driving. "Not much to do," he said, working the wheel to find an advantageous course. "I'd suggest going to the big jib, but the chute's still full. We're probably doing the best we can."

With Mona Light close abeam, Stu felt a bump that was heavier than from a wave. It was on the leeward side, and it seemed to push the boat sideways. It felt more solid than a wave, but it was subtle. There it was again. "Have a look," Andy said to Dugan.

With his light, Joe peered along the port side. "Nothing," he said, but he kept looking. "Wait . . . holy cow . . . you're not gonna believe this . . . it's a freaking whale! Damn near as big as the boat."

"Whales have been spotted in here," Damaris said as the whale made contact with the boat again.

"What else did you decide not to mention?" Sargent asked Damaris.

"What's the whale doing," Stu asked. "Is it love?"

"Hope not," Dugan said. "That could be a bit strenuous."

"Our bottom is white," Sargent said. "Whales are usually attracted by dark bottoms."

Teddy Bosworth poked his head up the hatch. "It's barnacles," Teddy said. "Whales often use boats for rubbing off the barnacles that grow on them. What kind of whale?"

"Big," Dugan said. "He, or she, is definitely rolling after she nudges us," he said, his eyes fixed on the whale. "Teddy might be right."

Teddy went to the rail. "Humpback," he said. "One of the smaller ones. Only thirty-five, forty tons. Forty feet maybe."

The crew was stunned into silence by Teddy's casual description as the whale's gyrations shook the boat. The smell of the animal was strong. The odor was more deeply aquatic than foul. It conjured the murk of low tide with just a hint of rotten lobster bait spicing the salty freshness of the mist of waves breaking on rocks. It was the powerful essence of a huge, well-traveled marine being.

"As an animal lover, I'd like to accommodate this guy's needs," Andy said as the whale continued to deliver solid bumps to the boat, causing the spinnaker to collapse for a moment. "He's a menace. We've got to concentrate on getting through here. Any suggestions?"

"We could poke him with something," Teddy said.

"I doubt he'd even feel it," Stu said. "Or it might piss him off."

There was a particularly heavy bump toward the bow that altered the boat's course by ten degrees.

Andy had gone below. He came up with the Very pistol — a flare gun — and a box of cartridges.

"I doubt those things will burn underwater," Dugan said.

"You got a better idea? Look, I never fired one into the water. I'm not sure I ever fired one, period. But they don't have to burn long. I think they go off hot enough to burn for a few seconds, which is all we need. The idea is to scare the shit out of this thing so she'll find another loofah for her beauty bath."

"He," Teddy said.

"Whatever," Andy said as he walked to the rail and looked down at the immensity of the animal that had been attracted to their hull. Forty tons — 80,000 pounds — was difficult to imagine. The boat weighed around a third of that. He walked forward to find the head just as the whale rolled and looked him in the eye. It was a sobering moment. Later, in an interview, Andy would say he had definitely felt awed by one of the ocean's mighty sovereigns. "It might not have been sex he was after," Andy would say. "The boys joked about that. But it was personal. He was taking care of his skin. It didn't seem wise to get between a whale and his toilet. Maybe it was because we'd been at sea so long, twenty-six days or so. When you are out that long you tread very softly. You're a speck on the ocean, a stranger in a strange land. The odds are so against you. You don't want to put out any bad vibes, like that ancient mariner who shot the albatross. He paid dearly. You mind your manners, observe the rules. 'Yes sir, Mr. Whale, your excellence.' And here I was, about to shoot at him, maybe hurt him. It was a bad minute."

Andy had fired. He made sure not to aim directly at the whale's eye and possibly blind him. But if he didn't fire near the head it made no sense. He had to get the animal's attention, and he succeeded. The flare had hit the water with an explosive burst, digging a hole and blowing water in every direction. The flare burned so hot it repulsed the water for a good five seconds before it yielded. But two seconds would have been all that was needed. In that short span, 40,000 tons of whale leaped away from the boat like it had been electrocuted. It dug in flukes as wide as the boat and with a mighty lunge disappeared, lifting a wall of foam that soaked everyone on the boat. The pointed tip of the animal's tail gave the hull a slap, leaving an abrasion.

Andy could never explain why he had reloaded the Very pistol. Must have been automatic, he said. But after a few silent moments while the crew was catching its collective breath, while heart rates subsided and calm returned to the boat, Andy would be glad he did. Stu had brought *All American* back on course. The spinnaker was pulling. Speed was back up to ten knots, with the bad chop continuing to punish boat and crew. Mona Light was now slightly behind them, with its powerful white beam sweeping across them every 2.5 seconds. It was on one of those sweeps that Joe Dugan noticed the disturbance in the water behind them. Something was coming at them at a fast clip. "Incoming!" Joe shouted. "Incoming!"

Andy turned, waiting for the next sweep of the light. He saw the bulge a sizable underwater object makes when it is moving fast, close to the surface. He aimed in front of the bulge and fired. Startled by the bright explosive flare, a good twenty feet of the enormous whale breached majestically from the water, seeking the sky. It wore a glistening cloak of water clinging to its massive body. The animal's angry eye above the pleated ventral, at the base of a powerful pectoral fin as long as twenty feet, seemed demonically fixed on them. The half turn it executed was frozen for a second, dramatically backlit by the next sweep of the light, before the whale landed with a resounding smack close behind the boat, a splashdown that displaced another foamy tsunami of water. *All American*'s crew, mesmerized, hardly realized they were again soaked to the skin. "Got it," Eric Menici said, cradling his video camera in its waterproof case.

That would be the last they'd see of the whale.

XVII

MIAMI

"No question it was Isha." It was Becky on the phone. "Looks very different. Blonde. Short hair. But I'd recognize that body anywhere. And the guy with her, RD, I'm sure, although I only saw him once that day you fired him, but it had to be him."

"Did they see you?" Andy was on the satellite phone.

"No. I'm certain. And a young girl. Maybe sixteen or eighteen, the three of them getting in a taxi."

"I'll be damned. Bad pennies. What in hell are they doing in Miami?"

"The girl had a Balenciaga tote bag."

"A what?"

"Those things cost at least three grand."

"Hmm. Isha found some money."

"My guess."

"Isha doesn't go anywhere without reason. But she and RD together, ho boy . . . how in hell?"

"Where are you?"

Andy barely heard the question. His mind was racing. Isha and RD. And money. Has to be a plan. Isha's plan. She's craftier than RD. Must have sought him out. Not hard. Mitch's guy. She'd have to know that. What do they have in common? Me. She should be in jail because of me. RD got fired off the boat, by me. But he got off easy. Mitch's thug. Could have had him busted and he knew it. He wouldn't cause trouble. But he could have been reeled in. By Isha. RD is a pushover for Isha. Now they happen to be in Miami just a day or so before we are set to arrive there. No coincidence. Revenge? My God. Are they coming after me? Maybe going after the boat? RD could get that done. He knows Lauderdale's seamy side. No, wait . . . It wasn't just sex driving RD. It was money. Mitch had bought him. Money! Andy felt a bad chill sweep over him.

"Andy . . . you there?"

"Yeah, yeah. We're a day or so out. Maybe eleven or midnight tomorrow. Listen, call Grady. You've got his number."

"Yes."

"He's in Miami. Waiting for us. He tracks our GPS. Describe our friends. Tell him we may be having company. See if you can find them. God knows what name Isha is using, but I'll guarantee RD is RD: Roger Davis. If they have money they'll be in one of the good hotels."

Isha, Jodi, and RD were sitting at a pub that had been

set up in Bicentennial Park, where the boats from The Race would soon be docking. It was their third day in Miami, and it was beginning to look like they had ventured down a blind alley. Jodi hadn't encountered any resistance when she had told her grandparents that she and Isha wanted to meet RD and *Orion* in Miami and watch the finish of a leg of The Race. Mark had been pleased that Jodi was starting to take an interest in boats. It was a given that Nina, her companion, would go with her. The two women seemed inseparable. Since Nina's arrival on the scene, Jodi had become a much more reasonable, manageable person. The Creightons' gratitude was boundless. And Mark had been thoroughly enjoying Nina's ministrations. When he had told them to hurry back as they were leaving for the airport, he wasn't kidding.

In Miami, the two women had moved into the Creightons' apartment at the exclusive Fisher Island Club. The club is located on the small island of Fisher at the entrance to Government Cut, a long channel into the city front past Dodge Island, where cruise ships berth. The Cut ends at Bicentennial Park. Isha and Jodi were transported by the club's launch, water being the only way to access the island. *Orion* had arrived at Fisher early that morning. RD had already commandeered Mark's RIB, which the club used when the boss wasn't in residence. In the RIB, the park was a ten-minute run.

Time was running short. The Race headquarters in the park indicated that *All American* had a sizable lead and was predicted to finish in the next thirty hours. Isha and RD had scoured the waterfront, called on all RD's connections, and had failed to come up with any reference to "Grady." The mood at the table was not good. Jodi was irritable, bored. She wanted to go to Parrot Jungle. Isha was just as irritable, eager to put a hit on Andy. The frustration of waiting was catching up with her, making her wonder what the hell she was doing wasting her time with this little bitch, flying around in stupid planes to ridiculous places like Mustique and now Fisher Island, for God's sake. She'd learned membership there was $250,000. To join a freaking club? She was feeling sick.

Becky had been busy. She'd struck out with the hotels, but she'd gotten lucky with RD. It hadn't taken her long to connect him with *Orion*, which quickly led to the Creightons, and she identified Jodi as the teenager she'd seen with the Balenciaga bag. She had tracked the Creightons to Mustique, and the boat to Fisher Island. Hidden behind a dark wig, big sunglasses, a Miami T-shirt, and cutoff jeans, Becky had hung out at Bicentennial Park, figuring that was where she'd find Isha and company. She was right. She'd taken a nearby table, where she opened her computer and sipped iced tea long enough to hear the word "Grady" spoken several times and to conclude that these campers weren't too happy.

Grady was incensed when Becky told him his name was being mentioned. He was also puzzled until Becky mentioned Mustique. "There's a guy there named Jocko," he said, "diamonds, very big player, goes both ways because it amuses him. Dangerous. The ones at the top are the dangerous ones. They feel disconnected, above it all, untouchable. They can let things slip."

"What should we do?"

"'We'?"

"I hate it, but yes, of course."

Grady laughed quietly. "Okay. Hang at the park. I've got someone. Let's whip them up a little for openers. My guy is husky. He'll be wearing a very tired Mount Gay hat. You can point him in the right direction."

Martin looked the part, hat and all. Everything about him looked salty: the frayed shorts, the old polo shirt, the worn boating shoes. He looked like he was born to crank a coffee-grinder winch. Or maybe play rugby. Becky saw him right away. They grabbed a table some distance from RD and Isha, ordered sandwiches. Then Martin made his move, walking past RD's table, making eye contact, stopping . . . "Hey, RD, right?"

"Hey," RD said, unsure but wanting to be open.

"Australia, nineteen eighty-two, Sydney Hobart, *Muscle Bound*. Right? Blew out two jibs the second night out. Did okay."

Martin was right. RD had sailed the Sydney Hobart Race in 1982 on *Muscle Bound*, an eighty-footer — Grady had provided that background — and when you sail with a crew of twenty, sometimes you don't even recognize guys from the opposite watch in the bar afterward. It can be embarrassing.

"Yeah!" RD said. "Hell of a race."

"Neville," Martin said. "Richard."

"Right, hey, Richard, grab a seat, have a drink; this is Nina and Jodi."

By the second beer, RD and Richard had replayed every sail change of the 1982 race, taking Isha and Jodi to the edge of consummate boredom. Finally RD was able to get to it.

"Dick, you're an Aussie — Sydney, by any chance?"

"My town, mate."

"I've been trying to locate a dude named Grady. My owner is talking about a charter down there next year, and people tell me Grady is the guy to see."

"Yeah, that's right. Grady. Sure. I can get a number for you. He's in Miami right now, actually. He's got a boy driving one of the race boats."

Isha had a mouthful of beer. When she heard this she nearly blew it all over the table.

"No kidding?" RD said. "Yeah, that would be great. What boat?"

"*All American*. They're doing well. Could win it."

"You're nuts!" Andy said to his father after hearing that he'd sent Martin to bullshit RD and tell him Grady was Andy's father, give him Grady's phone . . . Jesus! . . . and also what the hell! The next thing he could expect was a RIB full of armed thugs coming aboard to unscrew the fucking keel . . . damn! Andy was finding it difficult to whisper and yell at the same time.

"Not gonna happen," Grady said. "That would alert the whole crew to something very fishy going on. Then they'd have to kill everybody, and I don't think that's what they want to do. No worries. I figure they'll strike when you hit the dock at the park. First boat in, makes it easy.

Well done, by the way. I hear *Ram* died in the Doldrums. Nearly two days. Poor bastards. Better them than you. Okay, here's what I want you to do . . ."

After their bout with the whale, *All American* had negotiated Mona Passage without incident. The wind had decreased, as predicted, but they'd maintained enough headway to handle the nasty chop. They had finally broken free. The easterly had freshened as they'd approached the north side of Puerto Rico. From there it was a cakewalk around the Bahamas until they turned left for Miami at Spanish Wells. From there, the sixty miles to the finish a mile off the entrance to Government Cut was a joyride. The boys used the time to get the boat organized so no chores would prevent them from jumping ashore when they landed. The gun as they crossed the finish line confirmed they'd won the leg, and triggered a celebration on board. Good old Sargent produced a bottle of twelve-year-old El Dorado and passed it around. It was close to midnight. Only a few spectator boats were out. The engine was started. Sails were struck, flaked, and furled.

Andy got Grady's phone call less than a minute after they'd finished. He went below, as instructed, went to his bunk, which was located aft, under the cockpit, and lifted a corner of the mattress. There, as Grady had said, he'd found a small line he'd never noticed emerging from the bulkhead. Pull it carefully until you see the red mark, Grady had instructed. Andy did. Shortly thereafter, the engine began running very rough. Andy would find out later that he'd pulled a simple baffle partway across the engine's air-intake pipe. The device had been installed by Martin at the same time that he'd buried the tube of jewels in the keel. Grady had thought of everything.

Andy went back on deck. Eric, who was also the boat's engine guy, went below. He was back on deck shortly, shrugging his shoulders. "It sounds like it's not getting sufficient air," he said. "But there's nothing I can see causing the problem."

"Let's call Grady," Andy suggested to Sargent. "We don't want to get into the park and lose the bloody engine. He's out here. He'll have Martin with him."

Within minutes, Grady had brought his RIB alongside. He and Martin, with a tool bag, jumped on board. Grady gave Andy a hug. "Only one to go," he said. "Looking good." Grady and Martin went below. Having chased Dave Zimmer and Pete Damaris on deck, they raised the companionway steps in order to access the engine. Even though the passage was now blocked by the steps, they used flashlights, keeping the lights off below so those on deck wouldn't be blinded. Martin worked fast and efficiently. He removed the fake bolt top, pulled out the container of jewels. A new bolt had been threaded inside a steel tube that made up the half inch he'd widened the hole. He coated it with fast-curing steel epoxy and tapped it gently into the hole. He added a drop of solder. Ten minutes later, the engine suddenly smoothed out.

"What did you do?" Eric Menici asked them as they came back on deck.

"Magic," Martin said with a smile as he and Grady jumped into the RIB and slipped into the night.

✳

All American hadn't been tied up at the park for more than ten minutes before three customs officials arrived by RIB. They were friendly, welcome to Miami and all that, saying they knew the crew was eager to experience dry land after such a long leg, so let's get everyone checked in and get it done. They asked for all the crew to step ashore and line up with their passports. One officer handled that duty while the other two went below for an inspection. It seemed to take forever. After what must have been close to half an hour, the two men inspecting the boat came back on deck. They exchanged glances with the passport inspector, said all was good, and in short order the customs team completed its work and was gone.

As their RIB departed, Andy stepped on board *All American* and used the radio to send Grady a signal. He saw that the cabin sole had been disturbed. He hailed Sargent, who came below.

"They pulled up the sole. Must have been looking for drugs."

"Look here," Sargent said. "Every solder drop on the keel bolts has been broken. See the cracks?"

"That's amazing," Andy said, peering at the bolts. "Must have happened when we hit that container."

"Or maybe the whale," Sargent said. "I'll have the keel checked before the next leg."

"I think those customs guys were bullshit," Andy said. "Anything missing? You keep emergency cash, right?"

Sargent went to his bunk, rummaged around, found his toilet bag, opened it. "Son of a bitch. Gone. You're right."

"How much?"

"Thousand. In hundreds mostly. A few twenties."

"Grady's out there. He'll track them." Andy picked up the radio.

RD, Isha, and Jodi had the TV on in the Creightons' Fisher Island apartment and were well into their second bottle of champagne. It was meant to be a celebration, or so they hoped. The air was thick with the smell of Piton Pure. But no amount of distraction could combat the nervous state they were in. Sending RD's three crewmen to *All American* posing as customs agents was a mad idea. Isha's idea. She was convinced that a packet of gems would be found on that boat. It had finally come together for her: Captain Jerome confirming that private yachts were used as carriers, his mention of an Australian group that favored hiding them in the keel, and this man Grady, whose name she'd gotten from Sonny, who'd extracted it from Jocko — Grady who had turned out to be Andy's father. That part was a stunner. She'd never known. It explained a lot about Mitch, and Deedee, Andy's mother. No wonder Andy had been such a mess, and that Deedee had lost her mind before she'd lost her life. But this smuggling business was all too coincidental, definitely worth a shot. And there was really nothing to lose.

RD didn't like it. But Jodi was all for anything that sounded exciting, and the two women had prevailed. RD didn't have many cards. He worked for Jodi's grandfather, after all. Jodi could easily trash that gig if she wanted to, and it was Jodi who was basically underwriting this game.

Still, it had taken some seductive cajoling on their part, with promises of intimate activities implied. In that department, RD was no match for the two women. Passable customs uniforms had been created, and the RIB had been dispatched shortly after *All American* had finished. Now they were waiting, pacing around the apartment, getting high to calm their nerves, always a bad reason, and paying little attention to late-night television. Jodi had dozed off on the couch.

The quiet knock on the door was like a thunderbolt. It was Bob, *Orion's* mate. He stood there while RD and Isha stared at him.

"Well?" RD said.

"Nothing," Bob said.

"You checked everywhere."

"Everywhere. Spent half an hour below, just Alan and me while Bruce checked passports."

"The bolts?"

"Every one of them in place. Nothing. But I have to say we pulled it off. No questions asked." Bob stuck out his hand. "Hi, I'm Bob from customs." He grinned.

"That's just great, Bob," Isha said, disgusted.

"Thanks, Bob, good job," RD said. "See you tomorrow."

Dismissed, Bob left.

RD went to Isha, put an arm around her. "Hey, we gave it our best shot. Could have been right. What say we have a little celebration anyway?"

"In your dreams." Isha spun away, went into her room, and slammed the door, waking Jodi. "Wow, what happened?" Jodi asked.

Grady and Martin entered the Fisher Island marina an hour before dawn. They had the RIB at dead idle, moving very slowly, quietly. Another RIB was tied up alongside *Orion*, a RIB that matched Andy's description of the one used by the customs officers — orange with a tow bar and a Yamaha 250. They cut the engine, coasted up next to the other RIB, and slipped onto *Orion*. They went below directly, because their weight was going to move the boat enough to alert the occupants, and they wanted this meeting to be below. A night-light gave them their bearings. Three very sleepy-looking crewmen peered at them warily from their bunks.

"Oops, party's over. Wrong boat," one said.

"Don't think so," Martin replied. "Who's in charge?"

"That would be me," Bob said, leaning up on one elbow.

Martin sat on Bob's bunk. He grabbed Bob's forearm in one hand, Bob's hand in the other, bending the hand until Bob gasped in pain.

"This is gonna be simple," Martin said. "Give me the envelope with the cash you took off *All American* last night, and Bob won't have to have his hand replaced." Martin added a bit of pressure on Bob's hand to confirm his intention. Bob's body twisted. He choked in pain.

All three sailors were fully awake at this point. One of them started to speak. Bob let out a shriek that silenced him.

"Sorry, Bob," Martin said, "but I said this was gonna be simple, and I meant it. Or very painful for Bob. No one needs to talk. Just get the envelope and hand it gently to my friend here, and we're all good."

"Do it!" Bob gasped.

One of them got up, grabbed a manila envelope off a shelf above his bunk, and handed it to Grady.

"All there?" Martin asked.

Grady counted, taking his time, nodded to Martin.

"Okay," Martin said. "Good visit." Martin released Bob and stood up.

Grady started for the companionway stairs with Martin behind him. Bob had collapsed back on his bunk with relief, in pain, rubbing his wrist. The crewman who had given the envelope to Grady was still standing. As Martin passed him in the close quarters, he took a swing at Martin. Martin was ready. He spun and caught the man's fist in his hand, squeezing and twisting as the crewman howled in pain and fell to his knees.

"You should all go back to bed now," Martin said.

Martin and Grady got on their RIB and motored sedately out of the Fisher Island marina. RD, who had heard the motor start, had grabbed binoculars, but the bright stern light on Grady's RIB made identification of the boat or the occupants impossible. RD had no idea his "customs agents" had decided to relieve *All American* of its jukebox money.

XVIII

INK

Andy and Becky were lying in bed in their hotel room, replaying the past thirty-six hectic hours since *All American* had finished, winning the leg. They'd eaten a quick dinner downstairs in the interest of getting to bed early. Neither had had much sleep.

"I can't believe they would send fake customs guys to search the boat," Becky said. "And then they stole money!" She laughed, shook her head.

"Martin paid them a visit."

"That must have been something. Martin, what a character. Frightening. I wouldn't want him mad at me. He's the guy who 'tested' you, right?"

"Yeah. Still have bad dreams."

"He removed the 'package' right after you finished?"

"We faked an engine problem. He and Grady came

aboard. Ten minutes later, done. Amazing dude. Package is gone, thank heavens. But how'd you figure the young girl they had with them?"

"It was easy once I dug into RD. I probably found him the same way Isha did. I started looking in the big East Coast sailing centers, made some calls. He popped up. Got him connected to *Orion*, the Creightons, and their granddaughter, who has made the news a few times. Jodi. A handful. Isha must be connected there somehow, but don't know how." She paused. "I am so tired."

"Me too. Suddenly feel like I'm gonna crash. Very odd. Hope it's not food poisoning. I don't feel right."

Becky shut her eyes and pulled the blanket up around her neck. Soon both of them were fast asleep.

Becky woke up first. It was late. The sun was lighting up the room. Her head hurt. She looked at the clock — 10:00 a.m. Damn. How could that be? It struck her as odd that Andy was sleeping on his stomach. He was a side sleeper. She put a hand on his shoulder, gave him a little shake. He stirred.

"My head," he mumbled. "I didn't even have a beer last night. What hit me."

"Whatever hit you also hit me," Becky said.

Andy rolled out of bed, aiming for the bathroom. That was when Becky saw the thing on Andy's buttocks.

"My God!!"

Andy stopped, alarmed by Becky's tone. He turned. Becky looked very shocked, partially hiding her eyes behind her fingers.

"What?!"

She peeked through her fingers, aghast.

"You seem to have a tattoo on your butt. Seriously. I'm not kidding."

"Huh?" Andy went to the bathroom, craned his neck to see it in the mirror.

"I see something, and yeah, it burns a bit. What the hell . . . what is it?"

Becky was taking a long look.

"Well?"

"I can't believe this. It says, in quite large letters, 'FOREVER,' and there's a heart, and a signature: 'Isha.'"

Andy and Becky stared at each other, dumbfounded.

"That girl who served dessert," Andy said. "She wasn't our usual waitress. What the hell, Becky, you're laughing."

"It's either that or cry."

XIX

VENTING

"You did what?!" Cameron couldn't believe his ears.

"I had him tattooed." Isha had said it quietly. She didn't really know whether to scream it and do a little dance, or whisper it like an embarrassment. Revenge is like that. It can have a disturbing aftertaste. That was why she had decided to tell Cameron, to get it off her chest. It had seemed like a great idea at the time, the tattoo. Instant gratification born of frustration. But Isha needed to share the deed with someone besides Jodi, who was a murderer, after all. That had given her pause. A father and mother murderer. That was a bit much even for Isha. She'd gone to see Cameron as soon as she had returned to Connecticut.

She knew Andy's boat was carrying jewels. It had to be. The elements she'd pieced together were all too convincing. How RD's boys had missed finding them was a mystery. Either RD's incompetent, stupid crew had screwed it up or Grady had simply beaten them. How she hated to lose. For Isha, losing required an immediate response. Over breakfast she'd focused on the stars tattooed on Jodi's calf. She'd seen Jodi's tattoo a hundred times, but this time it had sent a message.

"Tell me more," Cameron said, collecting himself.

"It was easy to figure out where Andy was staying. He'd done some interviews in the Marriott lobby."

"Andy? Interviews?"

Isha cursed herself. She hadn't meant to mention Andy's name. She had no reason not to trust Cameron, but don't let it get out of hand, girl. Tighten up, damn it. What's happening to me, she wondered. The answer was evident: she needed to vent, and there was Cameron, a professional bound by ethical standards. Pull out his fingernails — that Hippo thing — and he wouldn't betray a client. Reliable Cameron, safe Cameron, with the reassuring artwork on his office walls, with the dreamy photos of him fly-fishing, walking with Chum.

"Okay. Andy. He's the target. Andy is the skipper and owner of a boat in The Race who's probably going to win it. Andy who stepped on me a while back before I met you at the rest area. Andy's who I was going after, am going after, because we're not done yet, goddamn it!"

"Didn't they just come into Miami, the boats in The Race? This was in Miami, this tattoo business?"

"Yes, after we failed to find the bit of cargo he was carrying."

"Cargo? On a race boat."

"Very small cargo. A little canister full of jewels.

Emeralds. Worth a million or more. So we thought. So I think! I know it was there. They just beat us."

"Wait. We're talking smuggling?"

"It's complicated." Isha was on a roll. "Andy only met his real father a few months ago. There was this vile man who had pretended to be his father for years, a vicious, mean-ass man I was working for. His stepfather. He had a grand plan to ruin Andy and take over the family business. Mitchell Thomas, who killed his wife, Andy's mother. I had nothing to do with that. He's locked up. Anyway, Mitch forced Andy to go on this race, and in Australia he met his real father, a boat guy named Grady."

Cameron realized his jaw had dropped slightly. "Go on," he said, trying to remain professional. "Andy stepped on you?"

"Another story. But we're pretty sure Grady has a little jewel-smuggling thing going on in Australia, and that he persuaded Andy to transport them on his boat. We had information about where the Australians like to hide such a package. And we had a plan. Get on that boat and search it right after they finished, posing as customs agents. We did. Found nothing. Either they beat us or I was wrong. Either way I was really pissed. We lost. Had to do something. Anything."

"The tattoo."

"Yeah. That doesn't finish it, but it sends a message." Isha smiled. "Took fifteen minutes. Will take a lot longer to laser it off. Or maybe he'll just wear it." She smiled.

"I expect there's a good story about how you had him tattooed. I doubt he would have accepted an invitation to accompany you to the parlor."

Isha laughed. "We managed to put a few drops of this powerful little drug in their desserts," Isha said. "It's good for several hours. Jodi doubled as the waitress. We had the artist lined up. Got the master key from the maid. Amazing what money will buy, isn't it? Jodi and I got to watch. I only wish I could have made Becky watch, Andy's girlfriend, his 'true love,' from what I gather. But I'm sure she's enjoying the end result. Pun intended."

"May I ask what the tattoo looked like?"

"'Forever, Isha,' it says. With a heart. And some filigree."

"Who's Isha?"

Another flub! "Isha . . . a nickname Andy called me," Isha said while cursing herself again. This truth thing was nothing but trouble. But it had worked with Jodi. "He said it meant 'pretty bird' in some language."

"I see." Cameron was suddenly on guard. This had been amusing up to now, with an agreeably sporting kind of moderate risk, dealing with this woman who'd picked him up on the Jersey Turnpike with her line of patent bullshit, this sexy little package of trouble waiting to happen who had managed to ingratiate herself with the mighty Creightons to the point that she was living in one of the cottages on their estate. Nina, now Isha, the welcome companion to the Creightons' troubled teenage granddaughter, and heaven knew what sort of deal she had with the old man — even the Creightons' guest on Mustique, of all things. But getting some guy forcibly tattooed, using who knew what manner of drug, and with this girl Jodi involved, in Miami, with jewel smuggling maybe going on . . . these were red flags flashing in neon that called for some serious reconsideration. Cameron had learned a long time ago that it was never a good idea to put confidentiality ahead of safety. He realized the fact that he'd bedded Nina, Isha!, a few times reduced his options. Calling the authorities was out of the question. Cameron knew he had to stay in character, or he might very well end up getting tattooed himself — figuratively, or literally. The thought made him wince.

"Well, this must make you feel a lot better," he said.

"What, talking to you?"

"Having tattooed your quarry."

"Both, actually," Isha said. "But like I said, we're not done."

"Oh, I know where to find her," Cameron said. "That's not the problem. The problem is what we're going to do with her. As I said, she managed to torpedo my better judgment. I can only caution you as a target."

Andy took another sip of his coffee.

"Men," Becky said, disparagingly. "I know what I'd do with her."

Cameron smiled. "I bet you do."

It hadn't taken Cameron long to find Andy. Andy had been putting in some time at Moss when he'd gotten the call from Cameron. There were only six boats in The Race, and only one skipper/owner with the name of Andy. The rest had been easy research: Moss Optics and the overpowering grandfather who claimed elves had helped him invent the big lens; the abused, frail mother; the news articles about Mitchell Thomas, the well-known amateur sailor and murderer of his wife, Andy's mother;

and Andy being forced onto The Race, with Moss Optics, led by Mitchell who was backing the first American boat ever. Andy had helped Cameron fill in the blanks and correct some of Isha's more creative stories. Becky had enjoyed telling of the bust in Mitch's Central Park apartment, when she had wrestled Isha to the floor as Isha went for an officer's gun. Andy and Becky had been amused by Cameron's lively version of how Isha had picked him up at the Vince Lombardi rest area, how she had found RD, and how she had landed herself a job as Jodi's companion.

The three of them had met at Paul's Pasta Shop in tiny Groton, Connecticut, a couple of hours up I-95 from Larchmont. As Cameron had explained, Isha was in the habit of showing up at his house whenever she felt like it. She had a key, he was slightly embarrassed to admit. Not a good idea for her to find the three of them having a chat. Cameron had chosen a place far away. He knew Paul, his pasta was the best, and Paul would let them use a little room upstairs where they could have privacy.

"You're the doctor," Andy said. "What exactly are we dealing with?"

"I think she's dangerous in a benign, mostly irritating sort of way," Cameron said.

Andy laughed. "In Uruguay a guy attacked me with a knife after she'd sent me to a very badass bar," Andy said. "She, or Mitch, had paid him. I took the trouble of going to see the guy in jail. He said she'd told him to kill me. That doesn't sound benign to me."

"I've had to sort through the many stories she's told me," Cameron said. "I do believe she's had a tough go. Early and frequent abuse. Probably from a near impoverished family. She's learned to use whatever cards she has to score some kind of a life for herself. She has some cards, and she likes a good life."

"She does have some cards," Becky said. "She certainly does."

"She hates men for good reason," Cameron said. "Thinks life is out to get her. Her first instinct is to strike out at people who get in her way, and ask questions later. She's incredibly devious because she's had a lifetime of practice."

"She's gotten to you a little, eh, doc?" Andy asked.

"She has," Cameron admitted. "She told me the other day about your bad years with Mitchell posing as your father. I could hear a little empathy in her tone. Just a little, mind you, but from Isha that resonated. Maybe it struck me because I had been so eager to hear from that side of her."

Empathy! Andy had to laugh, although laughing was the last thing he felt like doing halfway into his first laser tattoo-removal session. It was the first of six treatments — one a month for six months, they had said, to allow for healing. It was no fun, as the need for healing suggested. To require healing, one first needs to be hurt. Some "discomfort," they had told him. How Andy hated that word as used by the medical establishment. The word "pain" was obviously bad for business. Discomfort, some PR firm had decided, was more friendly. Much less frightening. It didn't matter what it was — pulling wisdom teeth, resetting a bone, relocating a shoulder, doing a root canal — there would be some "discomfort." You bet. The laser treatments weren't awful. The doctor had told Andy they wouldn't hurt as much as the tattoo, not knowing he had been thoroughly drugged for that little procedure. The indignity of lying bare-assed on a table while some technician burned away on his buttock with a laser topped it off. Better, he thought with a grim chuckle, not to know.

Andy had decided to have one laser treatment before the last leg of The Race began. In the tight quarters they inhabited, the crew would see his tattoo in the process of changing. He'd take plenty of heat about that. He'd have to think up some wild tale for them. But at least he could get Isha's name removed. That would have been impossible to explain. All the boys had seen Isha in action. Always best to let old news be no news.

"Ow!" Andy gritted his teeth at a particularly harsh burn. Empathy was the last thing he would have chosen to describe what was going on in Isha's head when she'd organized this little charade.

"Sorry," the tech said. "This thing with 'Isha' must have been a quickie. The ink is barely dry, as they say."

The tech, whose name tag read Janet, was attractive, but her eyes were cold. She wasn't quite up there with Nurse Ratched from *Cuckoo's Nest*, but she was cut from the same sadistic cloth. Janet was evidently into the punishment aspect of tattoo removal.

"Are you really sorry, Janet?" Andy said, resulting in another harsh burn. "Ow! For chrissakes!"

"No, not really," she said evenly. "I do enjoy my work, getting rid of these stupid things. I mean, why in the world would you do it, have some woman's name inked into you? On your buttock, in this case."

"I didn't."

"Oh, another drunk story. You were passed out and carried to the parlor by your drunken friends."

"Close."

"Really? Do tell, because I collect these stories. Maybe I'll write a book someday. I already have the title: Bad Idea at the Time. Like it?"

"Can't wait to read it. Soon to be a major motion picture. Aren't we about done here, Janet? Did you get 'Isha' off?"

"The question is, did Isha get off." Andy could hear Janet smiling.

"I'm sure she did," Andy said wearily.

"Oh, I can't wait to hear the details! We have plenty of time. Five more sessions to go. Almost done. Just now working on the A. Be patient."

"Ow!"

XX

GLORIA

In his office at Moss, Andy was making sure to sit on his left buttock while going through the stacks of reports and emails that had been organized for him by Gloria. Sam would have cut the pile in half, but Gloria was good. She was in one of her friendlier moods, partly the result of Andy having given her a raise large enough to result in cautionary calls from several board members. She had been pleased by the raise, but not overcome by it. Gloria's sense of her own worth was beyond anyone's grasp.

Reports indicated that *All American*'s participation in The Race was having a positive effect at Moss Optics. The attention The Race was generating was not only selling products, it was dragging a staid old company onto the public stage of commerce. While older board members observed the change with a certain amount of wariness, the attention had galvanized employees, making Moss a livelier place to be.

Andy was also encouraged by the progress being made on his old Mountain View project. No ground had been broken, but with the purchase agreement on the initial location having expired, the company was about to close on a much more attractive venue atop an accessible little mountain in Vermont. The project was being run, and run well, by George Cooper, the businessman with the meteorology degree whom Mitch had corrupted into absconding with the substantial personal funds Andy had set aside for the project. George had been found, busted, then forgiven and rehired by Andy against all advice. Andy had sensed George was no criminal. Mitch's offer, the cash plus enviable living quarters in Malaysia, would have been tough for anyone to refuse. And there was the ugly downside Mitch had threatened to create if Cooper had refused. George's gratitude to Andy would be lifelong, and his work showed it. Andy's old pal, the technical wizard Jeff Linn, was Cooper's right-hand man.

Gloria gave a preemptory knock as she walked into Andy's office with another folder of reports and correspondence. "Probably none of my business, but are you okay? You seem to be favoring your right side."

"It probably is, and yes I am okay," Andy said, marveling for the umpteenth time at how striking this woman was. She had her hair up as usual, but it wasn't just up; it was cantilevered in a clever way that defied gravity. And that was just the beginning. It helped that she was six feet tall, with excellent posture. The heels added another couple of inches. She looked down on the world from a gorgeous face adorned with prominent cheekbones beneath large, dark eyes working with a firm mouth that projected an intriguing challenge: truth or dare. Pretenders beware. And she was fit, with a pleasing, firm body suited for clothes mostly models could wear. Nothing fancy, very workaday, but always ready for pictures. The fact that she never wore makeup added a surprise that was somehow intimate.

As Gloria turned to leave, Andy asked her to stay. "Please, shut the door and sit down, if you have a minute."

Gloria shut the door. "I'm yours." She sat, looking attentive. Lucky me, Andy thought.

"When I rehired George Cooper, you were one of the few people on my side."

"True."

"And we were right, which was good luck."

"We were. It was more than luck."

"I have another situation. There's this person who has been a real problem for me. I finally have them in my grasp, and I really don't know what to do."

"May I assume we are talking about Isha?"

Andy lightly slapped the desk. "It's that transparent?"

"To me it is."

"Okay, that's on the table. Makes it easier. You probably know almost everything. But what goes on in here stays in here, right? In the vault."

"In the vault."

Andy quickly brought Gloria up to speed about The Race, about firing RD, and about meeting Grady, his real father, in Australia. He left out the jewel smuggling. He told Gloria how after a few months, Isha had surfaced at a Jersey Turnpike rest area, how she'd picked up Cameron and, after finding RD, had gotten a job with the Creightons as their granddaughter's companion.

"Apparently," Andy said, "Isha got this wild idea in her head that we had contraband of some sort on board the boat. She and RD, now a team out to get me for busting them — like I shouldn't have busted Isha for scheming with Mitch to ruin me and take over the company; or maybe I shouldn't have fired RD because he tried to throw me overboard in midocean? Anyway, the two of them appeared in Miami with the teenage granddaughter, who was obviously paying the bills to enjoy the show, to try and steal whatever mysterious item they thought we were carrying. Less than an hour after we finished, so-called customs officers showed up and searched the boat. They found nothing, so they made off with Sargent's petty cash . . ." Andy paused. "Sargent being the skipper."

"You have been busy," Gloria said. "I know Sargent. I send him checks."

"Having gotten all wound up for nothing, frustrated little Isha decides to take a shot. Okay, I'm gonna tell you something only three people know. That would be Becky, me, and Isha. Four: a technician. Everyone who is told a secret tells one person, right? I know that's true. But you mustn't. Okay?"

"Okay."

"Okay. At dinner, Becky and I were drugged. The granddaughter posed as a waitress and brought us drugged desserts. We get upstairs and pass out on the bed. I wake up in the morning with a tattoo on my ass."

Gloria burst out laughing. Andy glared at her. He might have expected it. "I'm sorry," Gloria said, still laughing, "I can't help it. Are you going to show me? Is that why you wanted me to shut the door?" She kept laughing.

"No, I'm not." Andy gave in. It was impossible not to see the humor in it. He managed to chuckle. "I'm already in the process of having it lasered off," he said. "That's fun."

"Oh, why?" Gloria said. "It's got to be a keeper. What does it say?" Andy had never seen Gloria so amused.

"'Forever, Isha,' with a heart and some filigree."

"Oh my word. With a heart. Where was Becky while this was going on?"

"Drugged. Passed out."

"She must love it."

"Yeah. She laughed too. Said it was either that or cry."

"Well, Isha had you where she wanted you. It could have been worse, you know."

Andy paused, studying the one-second pulses of the digital clock on his desk that matched his heartrate. He wondered why that had not occurred to him, that it could have been worse. A few possibilities instantly played in living color. They weren't pleasant. He found himself telling Gloria about Knife Man, the fight outside the bar in Uruguay, and how he'd gone to see Knife Man in prison. "He said Isha had told him to kill me."

"You, a white guy, an American, beat this local hired thug with a knife senseless, and he's in jail, all very embarrassing for him . . . of course he's going to say that."

"That's what Jan Sargent said."

"Well, Sargent and I agree. I met Isha several times

when Mitchell Thomas was sitting in your chair. She's very devious, a gamer, a thief, a scammer. But a killer? I don't think so."

"No offense, but she reminds me a little of you: strong-willed, determined, self-possessed, likes to do things her way."

"None taken."

"What am I gonna do with her? It would be easy to have her locked up. She's an escapee, don't forget, wanted, on the lam, and her association with Mitch would take many months to unravel while she was being held in confinement. Sending her down that road makes me strangely uncomfortable. She's got so much potential, if it could be focused in the right direction."

"That's a big if, but I agree. You have to figure out what's the right direction."

"Let's make that 'we.' Okay?"

"I've been thinking about it, actually," Gloria said quietly.

"Why am I not surprised? That's why you get the big bucks."

"Ever think about hiring her?"

"I have, actually."

"It could work. Not an office job. Special assignments. We have suppliers who get ugly from time to time. Disagreements arise. Situations. Executives playing hardball. Put Isha on it, send her to see them and negotiate. Our envoy."

"It could work," Andy said. "Worth a try. Got anyone in mind?"

"Yes, it's in the folder I gave you. One of our coating

suppliers is raising a fuss about pricing. Mr. Ogami. Very troublesome fellow, aggressive. Full of himself."

"Good test."

"I think so. And one more thing. Let me handle Isha. You set it up, then back off."

Becky was lost in space. She and Andy were spending a few days at his house in rural Connecticut while he put in time at Moss before he flew to Florida to rejoin the boat for the final leg of The Race. Andy hadn't wasted any time getting Becky settled behind the lens of the Moss Black Hole 949 telescope that took up half his living room. Jeff Linn had designed it. A section of the house had to be dismantled and rebuilt for its installation. A section of the roof had been made retractable. Andy had taken the dogs for a walk, purposely leaving Becky alone with the universe. Thirty minutes later, he'd kenneled the dogs and entered the house from the kitchen side as quietly as possible. Becky was still riveted behind the lens.

"Enjoying the view?"

Andy had spoken quietly. Even so it startled Becky, so transported was she. Not quite back to Earth, she stared at Andy, trying to regain her bearings.

"I'm speechless."

"It's just the moon."

"It's that word 'just.' I mean, how many hundreds of times have I looked at the moon, appreciated the moon for its mystery, adored the moon in all the silly, romantic ways. When they walked on the moon I remember watching that video when I was eight or nine, running outside to look at the moon, and running back inside again to see it up close, on TV. The moon . . ."

"That's why I picked it. It has quite an impact, seeing something so familiar in a stunning new way. Even the pros keep putting their telescopes on the moon. It's irresistible."

Becky shook her head, gently rubbed her eyes. "The images are so sharp. I'm so close to those mountains and craters, and those shadows! I'm there. I feel like I'm floating down under a parachute, that I could be landing any minute on the dusty surface. It's a great way to be reminded of the big picture, the really big picture. The universe, the moon, in contrast to all that stupid, short-term political stuff that ignores how we are wrecking our home, trashing where we live! Earth. You know I've read McKibben's book, *The End of Nature*. It is so clear, and so very scary about what's going on with trillions of tons of methane that could be released as the tundra melts, and the greenhouse effect warming the oceans, and the huge, catastrophic results those things will have on everything. McKibben says our habits, our economies, our ways of life have to change. But they won't. I wish every politician could sit here and look at the moon the way I just did. It might wake them up." Becky shrugged. "McKibben says it's already too late."

Becky went to Andy and gave him a powerful hug. "Thank you."

"And now the good news," Andy said. "The moon is just the beginning. The universe awaits. In a little while we can see Jupiter, maybe Saturn."

Later, as they were finishing dinner, Andy told Becky he'd had a talk with Gloria.

"Was Wonder Woman catching bullets in her teeth today?"

Andy shook his head. "I'm sure she could. She really is something."

"I know."

"We talked about Isha."

"Really."

"I brought her up to date . . ."

"Not the smuggling . . ."

"No, but the rest, the Miami craziness, the customs idiots, Jodi . . . the tattoo."

"Oh no . . ."

"It's in the vault. I trust her. She had a good laugh."

"I'm sure that would appeal to Gloria's sense of humor."

"Gloria also pointed out it could have been worse. 'Isha had you where she wanted you,' she said. I hadn't really considered that. Gloria's right. She did. The possibilities are not pleasant to contemplate. She had you, too. Lucky you don't have a tattoo."

"Ugh."

"Maybe I should check."

"Please do."

"Gloria thinks I should hire her."

Becky took a sip of her wine. "Really."

"Yeah. I had to admit I'd been thinking the same thing. It worked out with George Cooper."

"Isha's not George Cooper. George has a wife, two kids. She's got no responsibilities at all. That makes her a loose cannon."

"The idea is to give her some responsibility. Let her

know there's a legitimate place for her, that people think she's worthy."

"You are being so generous . . . after what she did to you, and I don't mean just the tattoo. You've already been quite generous to Isha, buying her that outsized chest. Where did that get you?"

"That was then."

"Okay. I have to admit some jealousy. Or maybe paranoia. She was your girlfriend there for a while, even though for her it was an act, a job. But still, there it was. And I understand there's something irresistible about her for men. Don't tell me if the circumstances were right she couldn't reel you in for old times' sake."

"Well, we would have to have lots of private meetings."

Becky picked up a roll and threw it at Andy. They laughed.

"Gloria said she would run her. Once I made the decision to hire her, I'd have nothing to do with it."

"Gloria running Isha," Becky said. "Wow. I suppose that's one way to keep an eye on her."

"It's either that or jail, and somehow that doesn't fit. She's never had a shot at the straight side. And frankly, the side I've got in mind for her isn't that straight. Gloria said she'd use her to go see troublesome clients and negotiate with them in her own inimitable way."

Becky laughed. "That's what I like about Gloria. She loves a challenge."

"You think it makes sense?"

"You're going to do it anyway. Just make sure your insurance is paid up."

"Practical. That's what I like about you."

✳

Isha was in Cameron's Porsche, which she had more or less taken over, cruising at eighty miles per hour on the Connecticut Turnpike, heading for JFK Airport and flights to some forgettable town in the middle of Wisconsin where they produced a vile chemical for coating the lenses produced by Moss Optics. It wasn't her idea of a good time, on the one hand. But it paid well, and she rather liked the prospect of a confrontation with some puffed-up executive, a chance to put some arrogant creep on his back where he belonged. And she didn't have much choice in the matter. There was that, like it or not.

It had only been a few days since her last talk with Cameron, when she'd found out the Hippo thing was bullshit. How had he put it, that his safety came ahead of a patient's confidentiality, words to that effect, meaning her ass instead of his, and that she was quite cornered. Not a good surprise.

She'd gone ballistic when Cameron had begun running it down for her, how he'd found Andy thanks to her stupidly blabbing his name — so much for the truth setting you free — and how he'd had a talk with him and that Becky bitch, the three of them sitting over lunch, calmly weighing her fate, the nerve of those pretentious assholes . . . She glanced at the dash and saw she was going ninety. She eased back to seventy-five, scanning the mirror for patrol cars.

Isha had let loose one of her better tantrums there in Cameron's office when he told her he'd ratted her out, crashing around the office at full cry, clearing his desk with a sweeping forearm, ripping several of those mollifying photos of Cameron and his goddamn dog off the wall and smashing them. Cameron had remained seated and unperturbed while she ran her course until she crumpled up on his couch in defeat.

Exhausted and temporarily drained, she'd heard him explain how, as a professional, he simply couldn't condone or withhold how she had drugged someone, broken in to his hotel room, and, while he was unconscious, had him tattooed.

"You mean as a professional rat," she managed to say. "And how do you condone our little sessions in bed? Or is that just part of your deal, screwing your patients?"

"I'm glad you brought that up," Cameron said, smiling. "This is where it gets good for you, because that's a foul on me. My hand is raised. Guilty as charged. It's not part of my deal, but it does seem to be part of our deal. And just so you know, I don't regret it. Not a bit. Normally, given what you did, I would have had to report you to the authorities. But you would have said I molested you, your word against mine, and, win or lose, it would have created a troublesome mess for me.

"There's more good news. Your old boyfriend doesn't want to bust you. He appreciates your talents, thinks you could shift into a new approach, make some decent money on a more straight-and-narrow, less underground track."

They weren't going to bust her? That had gotten Isha's attention. She'd lucked out big time when she'd managed to fit herself into that filthy heat duct in the Central Park apartment building. Being put into the system at this point would be a disaster, with all the junk they could think up to pin on her. Accessory to murder was for sure at the top of the list, and just getting around that could take years. "The system" was not a good option for Isha. But Andy? Andy was behind this? He didn't want her busted? That was astounding to Isha, and also somehow very satisfying. What a crazy card for him to play. It made her feel righteous that she'd gone against Mitch's orders and told Knife Man just to scare Andy, maybe cut him a little, but not to kill him. Andy didn't want to bust her! Amazing. She realized she was smiling. Why? Because it felt like a win.

When Cameron began to outline the specifics of the alternative Andy had in mind, working for Moss Optics, Isha wasn't so sure.

Gloria hadn't minced words. Isha appreciated that. Good news or bad news, she liked it up front in plain language, stripped of sugarplums and bullshit. She could count on a few fingers the people she knew who were that candid, and Gloria had just gone to the head of that small pack. It had started with a phone call: "This is Gloria Goulart. I work for Andy Moss. I'm calling to speak with you about employment." Direct and to the point.

The next afternoon they were sitting on a bench at Mystic Seaport Museum, Gloria's choice, on a slightly chilly, clear spring day. Even seated, Gloria was tall. That didn't bother Isha. At close to topping out at five feet three, in slippers, Isha had always found a way to use her diminutive self as an advantage. Since other women were almost always taller, she'd had lots of opportunity to fine-tune her small stature into a compelling attraction. But she had to admit that Gloria was imposing. She moved like an athlete. She was so composed. She projected such quiet confidence. Isha had seen Gloria a few times when she had gone to meet Mitch at the office, but this was the first time they had spoken. There had been very little small talk. Gloria had gotten right to it.

"You'll never come to the office," Gloria said. "You'll take on challenging associates and providers, people who are out to make a bit more hay than we think is appropriate. Special assignments. You would go see them, explain our position, convince them they should take a step back. I expect there would be four or five jobs of this nature a year. Andy thought you'd be good at it."

"I guess that's a compliment."

"It is."

"You know I have been living at the Creightons'. I am their granddaughter's companion."

"I do, and yes, we don't see why you can't keep that situation. That's up to you."

"Special assignments."

"Yes. First-class travel and accommodations, of course."

"Of course." Isha had to chuckle as Gloria laid out her future. "I guess I don't have much of a choice."

"That's true," Gloria said. "It's a very generous alternative to confinement." Gloria paused, glancing up to look at a bird perched on the complex rigging of the large, tall ship moored in front of her. "There is one very serious catch."

"Yes?"

"There will be no more interaction of any sort with

Andy, or Rebecca. None. If there is, this opportunity will collapse around your ears, and you will enter the system."

"I understand," Isha said. She looked Gloria in the eyes and added, "If you can catch me."

There was a dark moment before both women laughed.

"I look forward to working with you," Gloria said as she stood up and walked away.

"A piece of work," Isha muttered to herself as she watched Gloria's long, fluid strides.

Gloria was muttering the exact same thing.

The sign indicated that it was the last rest area on the turnpike. Isha took the access road and pulled the Porsche into truck parking. She removed her phone from her bag and stared at it. She pulled up the number she'd wrestled out of RD, and stared some more. She'd given it a lot of thought. It was time. She dialed. After five rings, she was about to give up when her call was answered.

"Grady."

"Hello, Grady. This is Isha."

"Isha . . . hello."

"Still in Miami?"

"Still."

"Good. Could we have dinner tomorrow night?"

"We could."

When Isha hung up, she was feeling good.

XXI

SAILING

It was remarkable how the weight was suddenly gone, how just the simple act of casting off was like breaking some umbilical connection, producing a ghostly silence where there had once been the chaos of all things land-based creating a benumbing white noise. You had to be casting off for somewhere distant for it to work, not just for a jaunt across the harbor or the bay, somewhere like Plymouth, England, a 4,300-mile trek from Miami that would take the better part of two weeks. Transatlantic. That would do. Unplugged, Andy thought, feeling bliss-fully untethered, venturing out where sea and sky were the only boundaries, where sun, moon, and stars, wind, rain, and clouds were the only companions. Other than the weather-fax machine and Andy's eleven fellow crew-men. But the machine was dormant most of the time, and the boys were untethered as well, free as birds, as high with relief as Andy was. In two hours, the last hint of land had disappeared astern. Priorities had quickly shifted to uncomplicated basics: course, boat speed, and if the proper sails were up and being well attended.

The start had been uneventful. In a moderate wind, the six boats had played it fast and tight for the cameras. Even if the start meant little or nothing in a 4,000-mile race, it was still a start. No skipper could resist the close combat involved, and television needed video and a story for that night's news. All six skippers went for it like it was critical. To make it interesting, a beer company sponsoring The Race had put up a $10,000 prize for the boat that won the start. Andy had not won it. Neither had Koonce.

After the start, Andy had gone off watch. Sleep had not come easy. It had taken a while to close so many files. With Sam's death, Moss Optics had become a burden. Andy had quickly concluded that the CEO job was not for him. He'd chair the board, have fun keeping track of the Mountain View project, but they had to find someone else to run the company. Another person for Gloria to handle. As if Isha wasn't enough for any one person to handle. Gloria had told Andy Isha's last words: "If you can catch me." What the hell was he doing, giving her a job, just being a sucker like all the other men Isha had manipulated along the way, damaging some worse than others, Andy thought as he scratched his right butt with care to temper the itch without causing discomfort. Discomfort. He had to smile. Just another monkey trained by Madison Avenue. He hoped Isha's first special assignment was challenging enough to keep her interested. If not? Well, she had a job. And there was Mark Creighton. She'd better watch herself with him. She might have met her match there.

Andy had tested his match with Grady. His last go-round with him had been on the tense side. Grady had another delivery in mind, a little canister that needed to go to the UK. Andy couldn't believe he'd suggested it after the angst involved with the Miami delivery once Isha had scoped it out. Grady had decided to stay in Miami to watch the start of the final leg. Andy had been talked into having a few friendly beers with him in Bicentennial Park two days before the start. Martin had joined them, which Andy thought was odd. Grady had gotten to it quickly.

"I thought you might like to take another little can on board," he'd said. "Needs to go to the UK."

Andy stared at his father, dumbfounded. This was going to be a regular deal? He was suddenly supposed to be a part of this group that had been moving jewels illegally for twenty years, this group that seemed to be run by Grady? The beer suddenly tasted very flat.

"No," Andy said quietly, shaking his head. "Nope. Not interested."

"You have to admit, the last one was easy. Piece of cake."

"Easy? For you. It wasn't on your boat. You didn't have Isha and RD homing in on you. And I've been meaning to ask, where did they get the information to start putting it together? They came mighty fucking close. Much too close."

"That's been fixed."

"What?"

"The leak. Guy named Jocko in Mustique. Big player. Does it for laughs. I told you the top guys were loose, dangerous. Jocko had a fall a few days ago. Broke his arm."

"Are you kidding?" Andy was stunned.

"Don't look at me," Martin said. "Never left Miami."

Andy wanted to run from the table. Somebody in Mustique had broken Jocko's arm?

"It doesn't happen very often," Grady said. "But you can't let that kind of loose talk go down without making a point. Would derail the whole deal. As it is, we'll have to go quiet for a year or so. But there's just this little can that needs to get to the UK."

"And the keel work has been done," Martin said.

Andy stared at the two men. "If you are here to persuade me," Andy said to Martin, "go for it." He'd gotten up and walked slowly away from the table. Five steps later he'd felt the hand gripping his shoulder, turning him. He'd clenched a fist, cocked the arm, then saw it was Grady.

Grady had looked at him. "My advice," Grady had said, "would be to stay north. Better winds this time of year, and the current will help."

"Thanks," Andy had said, and given his father a hug.

Becky couldn't believe Grady had tried to get Andy to carry another package.

"Oh, I can see it," Andy had replied. "That's what he does, and here comes a totally safe guy, me, his son — tested! — with one to the good, with the keel bolts prepped . . . why wouldn't he suggest another delivery?"

"Because you came too close to being ripped off, that's why," Becky said. "Come on! He's getting greedy."

"At least he didn't push it. I wasn't so sure. Martin was there."

"Martin." Becky gave a shudder, shook her head.

At 8:00 p.m. Andy went back on deck to take the wheel. The boat was quiet, close reaching in twelve to fifteen knots out of the southwest. Speed over the ground was nearly fourteen knots, thanks to an additional push from the Gulf Stream. Zimmer was trimming the jib, Sargent was on the main, with the Kolegeri brothers on the handles. They were favoring a northly course, as Grady (and others) had suggested.

Becky. She'd join him in the UK. She was the best thing that had ever happened to him. She was so . . . steady. Feet on the ground. And such a sexy woman. Teased him about being pregnant. She wasn't. Didn't want to be. Had taken the climate thing to heart. "Climate chaos," she called it. For real. This was no time to bring a kid into the world, she'd said. She'd gotten him into it. He had to admit, the science was impossible to ignore. There was a certain amount of cyclical climate stuff involved, true enough, but human involvement was huge. World population was increasing by more than 10 percent every ten years. Five and a quarter billion now. Too many hens in the pen. Too many hens who didn't give a damn, greedy little hens who could only protect their own little stashes of corn. Try to get more every day while the planet was being trashed. Denial, big time. He'd seen the extraordinary puddles of plastic in the Doldrums, garbage dumps a mile or two across.

Becky loved the idea of the mountain in Vermont, insisted they build a house for themselves there when

Mountain View went up. Keep our feet dry, she said. Made sense. They'd spend time in Europe after the finish. Becky had assignments. She'd volunteered to photograph glacial melting in Greenland and Spitsbergen on an annual basis for a big environmental group led by a senator named Al Gore who'd been preaching the perils of climate chaos since the 1980s. To mostly deaf ears. But Andy was in. It made perfect sense for Moss Optics to chip in, help make a difference. Moss, with its eye ever on the universe.

Jan Sargent had been below at the nav table. He came on deck, put his binoculars on the red light they could barely see a mile or more off to starboard. "Ram," he said. "Pay your money, take your choice. They go south, we go north. Wonder what he thinks he knows. Winner take all."

"You're even up with Koonce on the rum."

"Even up."

"Well, I hope we beat him. I hope you end up with a case in your trunk. But you know, either way is okay with me. Like those shirts Eric had made. Seen them? He plans to break them out at the finish. It says across the shoulders, 'Once you've been touched by The Race, life is never the same.'"

Sargent chuckled. "He got that right."

The smell of bacon cooking wafted out of the hatch, followed by Teddy Bosworth's smiling face. "Breakfast, anyone?"

THE END

Acknowledgments

The author would like to thank the following individuals for taking time to discuss various elements of the book with him:

Hannah Marie Blackwood

Patsy Bolling

Matt Collinge

Bryan Christy

Joseph Daniel

Anne Farwell

Dr. Philip Hirsh

Gary Jobson

Peter Montgomery

Mike Quilter

Bob Roe

Hamish Ross

Arsho Sarafian

Leigh Todd

Stephen Wilson

Peter Zukowski

Kippy Requardt, editor

Elizabeth Cameron, copy editor

Made in United States
North Haven, CT
02 May 2023